DARK BEFORE LIGHT

BY L. WAGNER

Dark Before Light

Linda Wagner

Published by L. Wagner, 2024.

Copyright

Copyright © 2023, 2024 L. Wagner. All rights reserved.

The characters and events portrayed in this book are fictitious. Any similarity to real persons, living or dead, is coincidental and not intended by the author.

No part of this book may be reproduced, stored in a retrieval system, or transmitted in any form or by any means, electronic, mechanical, photocopying, recording, or otherwise, without express written permission of the publisher.

Table of Contents

Dedication 1
Description 3
Chapter 1 5
Chapter 2 17
Chapter 3 31
Chapter 4 45
Chapter 5 51
Chapter 6 55
Chapter 7 63
Chapter 8 67
Chapter 9 73
Published Stories 79
Thank you! 81

Dedication

This is for my wonderful husband, who always illuminates my day.

Description

Warning: Adult audiences Only: Contains violence. Language. Not canon.

Embark on a journey to 1811 England with a captivating story that weaves love, intrigue, and the season's spirit. As London prepares for Yuletide celebrations, Charles Bingley relinquishes the lease for Netherfield Park. Fitzwilliam Darcy, impatient to see Elizabeth Bennet, seizes the opportunity to become the new leaseholder.

On Christmas Eve, Darcy, accompanied by his cousin, Colonel Richard Fitzwilliam, rides toward Netherfield with a single objective: to win the heart of the spirited Miss Elizabeth Bennet. As Darcy rides ahead, Colonel Fitzwilliam briefly halts in Meryton.

However, the path to love takes an unexpected turn after Elizabeth, Kitty, and Lydia Bennet venture into the woods to gather greenery for holiday decorations. Her thoughtless sisters abandon Elizabeth. Alone and vulnerable, Elizabeth encounters Lieutenant George Wickham, whose behavior deviates sharply from that of a gentleman.

In a tale where darkness threatens to obscure the light, Darcy must confront the unforeseen dangers lurking along a path in the wintry woods. Will Darcy's love prevail in the face of adversity? Will Elizabeth open her heart?

Explore the magic of the holiday season as Elizabeth and Darcy reach for a future full of happiness and joy. Netherfield Park is a place where Christmas miracles are destined to happen. Delve into this story, where the magic of the holiday season proves that the brightest light can emerge from the darkest moments.

Chapter 1

Out of darkness comes light: A quote derived from the Ancient Mayan Civilization.

December 24, 1811

The afternoon sun peeked through the stark canopy of the bare oak trees lining the side of the road that led to Meryton. Occasionally, a hearty pine tree cast a shadow across the thoroughfare. Mr. Fitzwilliam Darcy, accompanied by his cousin, Colonel Richard Fitzwilliam, looked forward to seeing Miss Elizabeth Bennet again at Christmas services. He was determined to win her heart and correct the poor impression he made at that awful Meryton assembly in September.

Richard watched Darcy through slanted eyes and teased, "Cousin, what are your plans for the evening meal? Does Netherfield have a cook? Any staff at all? I am parched and hungry. We should stop and get something to tide us over at the local inn."

Glancing at Richard with a faint smile, ignoring the suggestion of stopping at the inn, Darcy replied, "Indeed, Netherfield is scantily staffed but prepared to receive us. I have arranged for the cook to have a light supper ready upon our arrival, and we can relax after eating. I am eager to see the house and look forward to seeing Miss Elizabeth at Christmas services tomorrow."

Richard raised an eyebrow teasingly. "Ah, the mysterious Miss Elizabeth Bennet. You were rather voluble about her during our journey. Do you believe she will be at church tomorrow?"

Darcy's gaze turned contemplative. "Yes, she always attends services with her family. And I intend to show her a side of me she has not seen before. You know, the polite, friendly side."

"If you find that side, show it to me, too. I am used to the proud, disdainful, haughty-as-they-come persona you wear like a shield." Richard laughed at the astonished look on his cousin's face before Darcy laughed, too.

Twenty minutes later, the pair entered Meryton. As they rode down Main Street, Richard's stomach growled loudly. "I'm sorry, Darcy. I must dash into that tearoom I see up ahead and get something to eat. My gut wants fuel, and a good pastry will be just the ticket."

Darcy shrugged. "Do what you must. I won't keep you from refueling with a few lemon tarts. Just take the path to the left at the crossroads ahead. It goes straight to Netherfield."

Richard dismounted, saying, "I'll grab a few extra pastries for you, just in case your cook forgot about us."

Darcy rode on, eager to reach Netherfield, leaving his cousin behind. Darcy was anxious to present his best self at Christmas services and, perhaps more importantly, be in the company of Elizabeth Bennet. Her image danced in his mind as his stallion carried him closer to Netherfield.

Mrs. Bennet's enthusiasm for holiday decorations burned as brightly as the festive candles that would soon illuminate Longbourn. Today, she wished to transform their humble abode into a haven of Yuletide cheer.

"Elizabeth!" Mrs. Bennet exclaimed, her hands aflutter with excitement. "The house must rival Lucas Lodge in its Christmas splendor, but I've used all the mistletoe and holly. Go, take the basket, and fetch the finest greenery. Make haste, for Christmas waits for no one!" The mission was clear: gather mistletoe, holly, and an array of greenery that would drape their home in holiday cheer.

Elizabeth, wearing a fur-lined cloak and armed with a large basket and gardening shears, was about to leave the house when Kitty and Lydia, her two youngest sisters, volunteered to help. With an absentminded wave, Mrs. Bennet granted them permission, and the trio set forth for the nearby Longbourn woods.

Nevertheless, when they approached a fork in the road that led to Lucas Lodge, the promise of holiday merriment with friends proved too tempting for Kitty and Lydia.

"Lizzy, we will just visit Maria for a little while. We shall not be long!" Lydia called out, a mischievous twinkle in her eye. With laughter trailing behind them, they abandoned Elizabeth, disappearing in a flurry of skirts toward Lucas Lodge, leaving Elizabeth alone on the woodland path.

Undeterred, Elizabeth pressed on, her boots crunching on the frozen ground. The sound of her sisters' laughter faded, replaced by the silence of the woods. She tightened her grip on the basket, determined to fulfill her mother's wishes quickly. With each step, the imposing trees, stripped of summer foliage, cast elongated shadows that danced in the fading light of a cold afternoon.

Yet, the tranquility was fleeting. The woods seemed to darken as Elizabeth neared Netherfield's border in search of more mistletoe. Elizabeth, focused on her task, felt a subtle unease. Still, she pressed forward, determined to fill the basket with greenery.

Then, Lieutenant George Wickham emerged like a specter from the shadows a few yards down the road. Elizabeth felt a chill crawl up her spine as she held tightly to her half-filled basket, bracing herself to face the man.

As Wickham came closer, he cheerfully called, "Miss Elizabeth, what brings you to these lonely parts?"

Caution and wariness glittered in Elizabeth's eyes as she answered, "I am gathering greenery for Christmas decorations. If you will excuse me, Lieutenant, I have much to do."

Undeterred by her polite dismissal, Wickham blocked her path.

"Ah, Christmas decorations. A worthy pursuit," Wickham remarked, a sly smile playing on his lips. "But why venture alone? It's dangerous for a young lady."

Despite her composed demeanor, Elizabeth's unease flickered. "I can take care of myself, Lieutenant. Plus, this is Longbourn property. Why are you here?"

His eyes lingered on the basket she carried, then roamed to her figure, revealing a predatory glint. He ignored giving a reason for his presence. Telling Miss Elizabeth he was returning to the barracks after meeting a pretty widow in the Netherfield woods was not her concern. Instead, he redirected the conversation.

"Surely, Miss Elizabeth, you could use a strong arm to help you with that heavy load."

With practiced grace, Elizabeth sidestepped his advance, maintaining a safe distance. Wickham, however, persisted, his charm giving way to irritation. Elizabeth's instincts kicked in as he attempted to take her arm. She swiftly evaded his touch, her voice now firm.

"I appreciate the offer, Lieutenant, but I can carry this basket. Go away!"

Wickham's charm shattered, and his true nature surfaced when he lunged at her, attempting to grab her arm. Determined and unyielding, Elizabeth swung the basket at the scoundrel, hitting him square in the face.

"No!" she declared firmly. "I will not tolerate such behavior. Go away."

Wickham rushed forward, his face contorted in pain. He knocked the basket to the ground as Elizabeth evaded his grasp.

"Leave me be, Lieutenant Wickham!" she screamed, the sound piercing the stillness of the woods.

Elizabeth, recognizing that this man sought to harm her, began screaming for help while attempting to fend off his advances. The basket lay broken on the ground with its scattered contents. A blow to her face sent her backward in pain, stunning her long enough for Wickham to lift her and slam her into a tree. Then she felt excruciating pain as the back of her head hit the tree. Blood seeped down her neck as Wickham wrapped his hands around her throat and began to squeeze.

Dimly, she heard thundering hoofbeats, and out of the corner of her eye, she recognized Mr. Fitzwilliam Darcy charging his horse at Wickham with his crop raised.

A woman's desperate screams for help filled the air, reverberating through the trees. Was that Elizabeth? Darcy's heart pounded as he spurred his horse, racing toward the chilling cries. A gnawing dread propelled Darcy to push his mount harder when the screams abruptly ceased. He came upon a ghastly tableau. Elizabeth Bennet was in dire straits, fighting fiercely, valiantly resisting the advances of George Wickham.

His heart almost stopped beating at the sight of Elizabeth's tiny fists pummeling Wickham's chest, trying to strike a painful blow, kicking wildly at his legs, ineffectually pulling his hair. Wickham held her at bay, his face twisted into a devilish grin, his eyes gleaming with lust and malice. He punched her, threw her against a tree, and started choking her. The fiend was going to kill Elizabeth!

Darcy's horse, Thunder, charged directly at Wickham, snorting and neighing with fury. Darcy swung his crop with all his strength, striking an impressive blow to Wickham's face, then leaping from his mount unto the blackguard's back, forcing the reprobate to release his hold. Elizabeth fell to the ground, unconscious, her lips blue, her face and neck bruised.

Adrenaline, fueled by rage, coursed through Darcy's veins; he smashed Wickham's jaw with his fist and head-butted Wickham's nose, hearing it break as he crushed it. Blood spurted from Wickham's nostrils, staining his uniform. Darcy caught Wickham's left wrist as he dodged a blow and twisted it backward until it broke. Wickham howled in pain, but Darcy was relentless. He delivered another crushing blow to the jaw, sending Wickham down to the ground, then used his crop to strike a final blistering hit to Wickham's right hand, rendering it useless. Darcy turned his attention to Elizabeth, his anger replaced by concern.

Nursing the pain from Darcy's unexpected intervention, George Wickham lay on the ground, seething with humiliation and fury. The shock of being thwarted by his old adversary intensified the sting of defeat. Wickham's mind raced, searching for a plan to salvage his dignity, but he found himself at a loss, sprawled on the ground near the woman he had hoped to ravish. He cursed Darcy, Elizabeth, and fate, vowing to get his revenge one way or another.

As Darcy turned his attention to Elizabeth, Wickham seized the opportunity to flee. He was bloody and broken, with no wish to continue fighting; he stumbled away from the scene, blinded by anger, frustration, and pain. Thoughts of revenge filled Wickham's mind. However, fate had other plans for Lieutenant Wickham.

Colonel Fitzwilliam enjoyed the delightful offerings of the tearoom in Meryton. Lemon tarts and a hot cup of tea sat before him on the table. He savored the taste despite eating hastily. He chuckled inwardly, contemplating how his cousin's demeanor might soften in the presence of Miss Elizabeth, the lively and witty young lady who had captured Darcy's interest.

With a satisfied sigh, Richard paid for the treats and left the shop. He mounted his steed, Blaze, and continued along Main Street in the direction Darcy had pointed. The path to Netherfield was quickly located, and hoping to overtake his cousin, Richard urged his mount into a canter. He wanted to tease Darcy about his growing affection for Miss Elizabeth.

Alerted by screams, Colonel Fitzwilliam urged his horse to a gallop, halting when he saw a bloodied officer approaching. As the man got closer, the colonel recognized the blackguard. It was Wickham, the scoundrel who had tried to elope with Darcy's sister. Richard felt a surge of anger and disgust. Astride his war horse, a stern Colonel Fitzwilliam swiftly moved to subdue Wickham before he could slip away. Blaze responded to Richard's silent command to stop an enemy. The mighty steed crashed into the man's shoulder, spinning him around, then reared up on his hindquarters before delivering a forceful blow with his front hooves to Wickham's back, knocking the winded miscreant to the ground.

Colonel Fitzwilliam dismounted and grabbed Wickham by the collar, lifting him to eye level. He delivered a no-nonsense lecture on the consequences of poor behavior, his voice cold and authoritative. He accused Wickham of betraying his oath as an officer and dishonoring his regiment. He informed Wickham that he would never see the light of day again and then tied Wickham securely across the saddle of his horse, ignoring his pleas and threats, before striding along the path in search of his cousin.

Darcy's attention was consumed by the lady lying on the ground. Wickham's cruel assault had left marks on Elizabeth's neck and face; a small pool of blood lay under her head. Darcy quickly undid his cravat and tied it around her head, hoping to staunch the bleeding. Her shallow breaths and weak pulse indicated the severity of her injuries; she was alive, but barely. He kissed her forehead, whispering her name and praying she would be well. He felt a surge of love and guilt, wishing he had confessed his feelings, returned sooner, and protected her from Wickham's evil designs.

Richard arrived just as Darcy was lifting the sweet burden from the ground. He saw the unconscious woman and, surmising it was Darcy's beloved, felt a pang of sympathy for his cousin. The colonel knew how much Darcy cared for Miss Elizabeth and how much this must hurt him. He also saw the blood and bruises on Darcy's forehead and felt a surge of admiration for Darcy's courage and strength. He saw the blood-soaked riding crop, picked it up, and stowed it on the saddle.

"Darcy, let me help you. Give her to me while you mount your horse," ordered the colonel as if he were speaking to a recruit under his command.

Darcy, his soul tormented by Elizabeth's condition, without a word, complied. Once Darcy settled in the saddle, Richard handed the young lady to his cousin. Moments later, Elizabeth was safely cradled against his chest; he rode to Netherfield, the nearest refuge, rather than risk the longer journey to Longbourn. Quickly getting Elizabeth's injuries treated was imperative. His heart, typically guarded and reserved, was laid bare as he prayed the woman he longed to marry would recover from this ordeal.

After placing Elizabeth in Darcy's arms, Colonel Fitzwilliam wasted no time delivering Wickham to the militia's brig in Meryton, where he would face the consequences of his assault on Miss Elizabeth. The townspeople witnessed the rogue's fall from grace as the officer was brought into town tied to the back of a horse like a common criminal. The sound of jeers filled the air as Wickham hung his head in shame, his face bruised and bloodied. He felt the eyes of the people he had deceived burning into his skin.

The news of Wickham's downfall spread quickly through Meryton, marking the end of his popularity in the town. As the door to the militia's brig clanged shut behind him, Wickham faced the repercussions of his misdeeds in the cold confines of a cell. He shivered as he lay on the hard cot, his only companions the rats and the flies. Cursing his fate and his foolishness, Wickham wondered if a surgeon would come to tend his wounds or if he would rot in this hellhole.

Having delivered his prisoner to the brig, Colonel Fitzwilliam ordered a soldier to fetch a medic for Wickham and strode toward the commander's office.

Colonel Forster, the commanding officer of the local militia regiment, stood to greet his old school chum as Colonel Fitzwilliam entered the office. Colonel Forster's eyes reflected his concerned curiosity. It was rare that a highly decorated officer from the regulars visited a militia commander.

"Colonel Fitzwilliam," Colonel Forster acknowledged. "What brings you here today? It's been a long time since our days at Cambridge."

After a polite greeting, Colonel Fitzwilliam wasted no time recounting the shocking events that had just transpired on the outskirts of Meryton. He detailed George Wickham's vicious assault on Elizabeth Bennet, emphasizing the severity of the situation and the need to protect the young lady's reputation.

"I apprehended Wickham fleeing the scene and brought him to town securely bound on my horse. My cousin, Mr. Fitzwilliam Darcy, is adamant that Wickham face justice for his assault on Miss Elizabeth unless charges with greater gravity can be filed," Colonel Fitzwilliam declared, his voice firm and resolute.

Colonel Fitzwilliam clenched his jaw as he recalled the sight of scattered greenery and the remains of a straw basket lying on the ground near a battered Elizabeth Bennet. He felt a surge of anger and disgust at the man who had dared to harm the young lady and a pang of guilt for not being there sooner to deliver a few crushing blows to the miscreant.

Colonel Forster's stern gaze fixed on Colonel Fitzwilliam as he processed the seriousness of the situation. "Assaulting a gentlewoman is a grave offense, Colonel Fitzwilliam. We cannot tolerate such behavior within our ranks. I will investigate the man's daily activities. Everything possible will be done to protect the lady's identity and reputation."

Frowning at the thought of the scandal if the lady's identity was discovered, Colonel Forster inwardly groaned in vexation. He knew that Wickham's antics at the local pub had already tarnished the militia's reputation and that this crime would only worsen matters. Feeling sorry for the innocent victim, who had suffered at the hands of a scoundrel, Colonel Forster resolved to do his duty and bring Wickham to justice.

Colonel Fitzwilliam, exasperated, said, "I suggest you have a chat with the local shopkeepers. Wickham is notorious for racking up debt and fleeing when the collectors arrive. If the militia cannot find suitable reasons to end this man's aberrant behavior permanently, Mr. Darcy will have the civil authorities take him to Marshalsea for nonpayment of debt."

Colonel Forster, his eyes widening in disbelief, gasped, "What? Everybody believes Wickham was cheated out of a living by Mr. Darcy. Is that a lie, Colonel Fitzwilliam?" The commander had believed Wickham's tales and sympathized with his plight. He had even defended him against those who claimed the man was spinning a story of woe to garner sympathy from the ladies. Shock and betrayal washed over him as he realized a practiced liar had fooled him.

"Colonel Forster," thundered Richard, "the man you believed without proof owes over two thousand pounds in unpaid bills!" He began pacing around the room before stopping in front of Forster's desk and slamming a fist down.

Richard blasted the air between the two men; his voice was deafening. He spat out, "My uncle, George Darcy, sent Wickham to Cambridge and never understood the man's unsuitability for the church. His will left Wickham a thousand pounds unconditionally. Wickham claimed he wanted to study law. He relinquished all rights to the living. The blackguard signed legal documents witnessed by the executor, Mr. Fitzwilliam Darcy, three solicitors, a judge, and me. He received three thousand pounds to compensate for the loss of the living immediately after the signatures were placed on the paper. He spent or gambled away four thousand pounds in three years. Would you put such a man in charge of a congregation if he returned to you when the incumbent died with his demand for the living, even though he never took orders and lived a depraved life?"

Based on Colonel Forster's dumbfounded expression, the question would go unanswered. As Colonel Forster realized the extent of Wickham's duplicity, a cold sweat formed on his forehead, and he felt a surge of shame and remorse for having trusted such a scoundrel. He wondered how many people were fooled by Wickham's charm and lies.

Colonel Fitzwilliam added, "I have placed Wickham in the militia's brig and sent the medic to him. I suggest you search his quarters. He likes to steal things that take his fancy. He must face the consequences of his actions."

With a steely glint in his eyes, Colonel Richard Fitzwilliam warned, "Commander, do not be lenient. This man has been preying on people his entire life."

Colonel Forster nodded, acknowledging Colonel Fitzwilliam's request. "Very well. I will ensure a fair and just process. Such misconduct reflects poorly on the entire regiment, and we cannot allow it to go unpunished."

"I heartily agree, sir. Do you wish to speak with my cousin?" Colonel Fitzwilliam asked, his tone softening slightly. Since Wickham's injuries required medical attention, he knew that his cousin must explain the events and that they would need Colonel Forster's cooperation.

Colonel Forster, after a moment of contemplation, nodded. He had to question Mr. Darcy. The militia's commander hoped that Elizabeth Bennet's injuries were being exaggerated. He would have to see the young lady.

"We cannot afford any scandal tarnishing the militia's reputation. Join me for dinner. After, you can escort me to Netherfield to interview Mr. Darcy."

Colonel Fitzwilliam and Colonel Forster left the office together, determined to give Wickham everything he deserved.

Chapter 2

Sitting alone in his study, contentedly reading a new poetry collection, ignoring the clock on the mantle, relishing the relative quiet with his youngest daughters out of the house with Lizzy, all was calm, a miracle granted from the heavens in a place where the Roman goddess, Discordia, often ruled.

His peace was momentarily disturbed when Mrs. Hill brought him an urgent message from Netherfield Park. He took the message and tossed it onto his desk. He did not read correspondence of any kind in front of servants.

"Did the man wait for a reply?" he asked with a lifted brow and a glance at the clock. What could be urgent at 1:45 in the afternoon?

"No, sir. He said he had to get to Meryton to find Mr. Jones for his master. He galloped down the driveway. Something serious must have happened," speculated the housekeeper. She left the study quickly as the front door opened and slammed shut, forgetting to close the study door.

Just as Mr. Bennet reached for Netherfield's sealed message, the sounds of boisterous chatter reached his ears. Kitty and Lydia, his two youngest daughters, were home, their voices competing to be heard.

"Mama, Lizzy will be here any minute! She collected the most splendid greenery for decorating Longbourn, but we forgot to bring shears, and Lizzy would not let us borrow hers, so our basket is empty," Lydia announced with an air of unconcern.

Mr. Bennet, distracted by the noisy entrance of his daughters, went to the parlor and watched as the girls deposited an empty basket on a table. The message was pushed to the back of his mind as the lively banter of his daughters filled the room. Eventually, he returned to his study and lost himself in his book, forgetting to read the message.

Two hours later, Mrs. Bennet, in a flurry of agitation and frustration, stormed into Mr. Bennet's study, her countenance expressing displeasure.

"Mr. Bennet, where is Lizzy? She was supposed to be back hours ago! My plans for additional decorations are ruined. The sun will set soon, and she did not take a lantern. You must find her and bring her back immediately!" Mrs. Bennet demanded, her voice a blend of irritation and distress.

Kitty and Lydia, now subdued and remorseful, exchanged guilty glances. Mr. Bennet's expression darkened as he realized Lizzy was alone in the woods.

Mr. Bennet's tone, disappointed and angry, asked, "What is the meaning of this? Were you or were you not with Lizzy gathering greenery?"

Kitty stammered, "We left her at the crossroads to Lucas Lodge, Papa. We were in such a hurry to..."

Lydia interrupted, "But Lizzy said she would bring the greenery. We thought it would be enough!"

Darkness was approaching, so he dismissed his wife and wayward daughters with a stern glare.

"A hurry to go where? Never mind, you will tell me later. Leave me. I must find Lizzy."

Once the ladies left the room, Mr. Bennet, alone once more, sighed deeply, eyeing the unopened missive lying on his desk with trepidation. He resolutely picked up the note from Netherfield, a sinking feeling settling in his stomach; he could not shake the worry that the urgent matter might be connected to Lizzy's absence. He broke the seal and swiftly read the succinct note.

Netherfield Park - 1:30 pm

December 24, 1811

Mr. Bennet, please excuse this interruption on Christmas Eve. You must come to Netherfield <u>immediately</u>. Events have transpired this afternoon that <u>require</u> your attendance. I cannot put more in writing. Please come <u>quickly</u>.

Regards,

Fitzwilliam Darcy

After throwing the letter into the fire, Thomas Bennet rushed from his study, ordered his carriage, donned his winter coat, and began praying that his daughter was alive and unharmed. His mind filled with speculation during the short trip to Netherfield, and by the time he arrived, Mr. Bennet was furious at his wife, his two youngest daughters, and Mr. Darcy.

The flames in the fireplace danced wildly, casting eerie shadows across Fitzwilliam Darcy's face as he sat alone in the study at Netherfield Park. His usually composed countenance displayed a potent mix of anger, distress, and a thirst for vengeance. A wayward lock of hair fell across his forehead, partially covering the bruise he had received when crashing it into Wickham's nose. His eyes burned with a dark fire, and his lips pressed into a thin line. The pain in his side, where Wickham landed a solid blow, still pulsed through his body.

His hands clenched into fists, and his jaw tightened as he brooded over the imminent confrontation with Mr. Bennet. It was past 3:30, two hours after he sent a message to Longbourn, and the Bennet patriarch was still not here.

Darcy's mind raced with ideas for handling the man, fully aware that their meeting would be distasteful at best or volatile at worst. The selfish indolence of the Longbourn patriarch was only surpassed by the scathing comments he spewed at his foolish wife. Darcy wondered how such a man could have fathered a woman like Elizabeth, who had captivated his heart with her wit, beauty, and courage.

Darcy's harsh breathing, indicating the ragged state of his thoughts, broke the silence until the distant sounds of rapidly approaching footsteps interrupted his contemplation. Mr. Bennet had arrived, and the impending confrontation hung like an unspoken challenge. Darcy braced himself for the inevitable clash, hoping to resolve the matter as quickly and civilly as possible for Elizabeth's sake.

The door to the study crashed open; there was no knock, no waiting for the butler to announce the visitor. The incivility of the intruder spoke volumes; Mr. Bennet entered with a determined stride, his brows furrowed with frustrated worry. He looked sternly at Darcy, who rose from his seat, his tall, muscular frame imposing in the dimly lit room. Darcy felt a surge of resentment at the man's lack of manners, but he suppressed it and greeted him with cold politeness before firmly shutting the door.

"Mr. Darcy!" Mr. Bennet's voice was almost accusatory. "What in blazes is the meaning of your note? What is this matter you wish to discuss on Christmas Eve? Is it about my daughter, Lizzy?"

Darcy's jaw clenched even tighter as he met Mr. Bennet's gaze head-on. "Calm yourself, sir. This is a delicate matter. I could not put the specifics in my message because I do not know these servants well enough to trust their discretion. Miss Elizabeth is upstairs, receiving the care she sorely needs from Mr. Jones." He hoped his words would reassure the man, but he saw no relief in his eyes, only suspicion and anger.

Mr. Bennet's eyes narrowed, voice rising in volume and pitch. He demanded, "And what care might that be? What happened to her?"

The flames in the fireplace flared higher, mirroring the situation's intensity. Darcy took a measured breath before responding. He knew he had to tell the truth but dreaded the reaction it would provoke. Darcy wished to spare Mr. Bennet the shock of hearing what had befallen his daughter, but there was no choice; he must enlighten Longbourn's patriarch about the situation and the consequences.

Darcy spoke calmly and clearly, but his eyes betrayed his fury and anguish. "On my way to Netherfield, I heard screams from the forest. I followed the sounds and found Miss Elizabeth under attack by Lieutenant George Wickham on one of the trails. In her struggle with the blackguard, she sustained several injuries before I could intervene. Once at the scene, I fought Wickham, ran him off like the dog he is, and brought your unconscious daughter here to Netherfield for medical attention. At the same time, my cousin, Colonel Richard Fitzwilliam, who was a few minutes behind me on the road, apprehended the fleeing wastrel and took the villain to the militia camp in Meryton."

Mr. Bennet's eyes widened in disbelief; he moved closer to Darcy, his face red with rage, and shouted, "Lieutenant George Wickham? I knew he was a flirt, but I never thought he would stoop so low. Perhaps my daughter came upon the two of you fighting over his lost inheritance. Maybe she tried to stop you from injuring the lieutenant! Explain yourself, man!"

Darcy forced his fists to unclench, but the tension in his shoulders remained palpable. Elizabeth's father was not stupid. Was it necessary to spell out the villain's nefarious intentions? Indeed, Darcy would not go into explicit details with the man. He did not want to sully Elizabeth's reputation or expose her to further humiliation. Mr. Bennet's temper was already on the verge of exploding. He decided to be as brief and vague as possible, hoping Mr. Bennet would read between the lines.

Darcy's tone was severe, and his gaze was accusatory when he spoke. "Wickham betrayed your trust and sought to harm Miss Elizabeth. I could not ignore her plight. There is naught else to explain unless you wish to enlighten me as to why your daughter was walking unescorted so far from your home on a secluded forest path or, worse, escorted, with your approval, by a rake you entertain in your home." Darcy's words were like a slap in the face to Mr. Bennet, who cringed at the reproach.

Mr. Bennet swallowed hard and said defensively, "Mrs. Bennet asked Elizabeth to gather greenery for the Yuletide decorations. Kitty and Lydia accompanied her from the house and were returning when I got your note. They claimed Elizabeth was closely following." Mr. Bennet, chagrined and mortified that his two youngest girls had lied to him, wondered when the girls abandoned their sister. He felt a pang of guilt and remorse, knowing that he had indulged their whims and follies too much and that he had failed to protect his most precious child.

Darcy's eyes flashed angrily, and he snapped, "It has been almost three hours since I came across Lieutenant Wickham assaulting Miss Elizabeth on that path. Upon reaching Netherfield, the housekeeper, Mrs. Nichols, took charge of your daughter and settled her in a guestroom with a maid's help. Afterward, I sent an urgent note to Longbourn asking you to come here, indicating a matter of grave importance that needed your immediate attention. The messenger rushed to Meryton, found Mr. Jones, and brought the man to Netherfield. The apothecary has been here since 2 o'clock."

Pacing in agitation, Darcy paused briefly to gather his thoughts. The vociferous fury on display by such a taciturn man shocked Mr. Bennet.

Darcy's insulting denunciation continued, "I knew you were indolent, sardonic, and rude but never thought you gullible enough to believe the polished lies of a dissolute rakehell, especially when your brother-in-law is a solicitor. Clearly, you ignored my note for hours. Since my servant assured me that he saw the return of your youngest daughters as he was leaving your property, when did the prolonged absence of Miss Elizabeth give you enough incentive to put down your book and get out of your favorite chair? What finally caused you to come here?" Darcy's livid countenance was far from the stoic demeanor usually seen by the citizens of Meryton.

A heavy silence hung in the air as the two men locked eyes, each grappling with the harsh truths the angry young man delivered. Suddenly, there was a knock on the door, and the apothecary, Mr. Jones, entered the study without waiting for an invitation.

"Mr. Darcy," Mr. Jones addressed him with a nod. "Miss Bennet is alive, but her injuries are severe. She will need rest, quiet, and careful attention for at least six weeks. Based on the laceration on the back of her head, your guest may have a severe concussion. There are no obvious broken bones, but when she regains consciousness, I must speak with her to determine if there are any fractures or sprains. She cannot leave Netherfield without risking further injury." Mr. Jones looked between the two men, felt the hostility in the room, and swiftly returned upstairs to his patient, completely ignoring the Bennet patriarch.

Darcy saw the anguish in Mr. Bennet's eyes and felt a twinge of pity for the man. He softened his tone, offering comfort to Mr. Bennet.

"Miss Elizabeth is a strong and brave woman. I am certain she will recover from this ordeal. She is not alone since Mr. Jones and a maid are with her. When you see her, try to act normally. I must warn you the bruising and swelling on her face and throat is extensive…Wickham hit her face…with his fist…he was… choking her." Involuntarily, Darcy shuddered.

Mr. Bennet nodded, blinking the moisture from his eyes. He was grateful for Darcy's kindness and eager to see his daughter to assure himself that she was alive and safe. He said, "Thank you for saving my daughter's life and for bringing her here. You have done more than I deserve and more than I can ever repay. You have shown yourself to be a true gentleman. I apologize for my behavior."

Darcy was surprised and touched by Mr. Bennet's words. He had not expected such a change of heart or a display of emotion. Darcy's gaze never wavered from Mr. Bennet and said, "You owe me nothing, sir. I only did what any man of honor would do. And you have nothing to apologize for. I have been rude to you and did nothing to earn your esteem. I am the one who should beg your pardon."

Mr. Bennet, after a contemplative pause, sighed heavily. "Let us go to my daughter. We can discuss this further after I have seen her."

Darcy nodded, the weight of the dreadful incident pressing heavily on his heart. He dreaded the upcoming encounter with Elizabeth, yearning for her wakefulness yet fearing her possible reluctance to stay at Netherfield. Convincing Mr. Bennet to remain for propriety, possibly in the company of another female relative, could pose a challenge. He fervently wished that Elizabeth would agree to marry him before realizing she would be ruined if she did not.

Upstairs in the best guestroom, Elizabeth Bennet lay in bed, her vibrant spirit temporarily defeated by the events that had transpired earlier. A flustered maid bustled around the patient under the watchful eye of Mr. Jones, applying a salve to Elizabeth's hands. Candles flickered, casting a soft glow on Elizabeth's swollen, bruised face. Her eyes began fluttering as consciousness slowly returned; her first waking thoughts were of the handsome man who came to her rescue, followed by the excruciating pain in her head when she tried to turn it. She whimpered.

The maid and a profoundly concerned Mr. Jones hovered nearby. As Darcy and Mr. Bennet entered, Elizabeth's eyes met Darcy's, and a fleeting expression of relief passed between them. The atmosphere in the room seemed to shift. Elizabeth's wakefulness promised a healthy future, and the look in her eyes perhaps a change of heart.

"Mr. Darcy? Papa? Where am I?" Her raspy, weak voice reflected her confusion and demonstrated the severity of the injury to her throat.

Darcy stepped forward, his worry etched on his face. "Miss Elizabeth, you are safe now. Wickham is gone. This is Netherfield. You sustained serious injuries, but Mr. Jones is attending to you, and your father has come."

Elizabeth's brow furrowed as the memories of the confrontation with Wickham flooded back. She winced, feeling the pain from her injuries. A low moan escaped her lips. Fear and anxiety overtook her senses. "Wickham...gone? Netherfield?"

Her bandaged hand flew to her throat where the imprint of Wickham's hands was purpling, and her gaze flickered between Darcy and her father, piecing together the events. Tears welled in her eyes and spilled over to run down her cheeks. The maid, murmuring comforting sounds, gently wiped them away with a soft cloth. Then the woman poured Elizabeth a cup of willow bark tea with honey, holding it to her lips, urging the injured lady to drink it. Elizabeth drank the beverage slowly, appreciating the copious amount of honey that masked its bitter taste.

Mr. Bennet, standing at the side of her bed, sighed heavily. The man was reeling from the sight of his battered daughter, reaching out a finger to brush a wayward lock of hair from her disfigured face; the finger was immediately withdrawn when she flinched. He spoke slowly, "Elizabeth, it seems Mr. Darcy saved you from Lieutenant Wickham. We will talk later; focus on your recovery."

Elizabeth nodded weakly, wincing from the acute pain the simple gesture caused, her eyes returning to Darcy's. "Thank you," she whispered, her voice filled with a vulnerability that surprised everyone.

Mr. Jones indicated the men should leave the room so he could finish the examination. They left Elizabeth with reluctance, but the stern glance of the apothecary toward the door ordered them to leave.

In the hallway outside Elizabeth's room, Darcy and Mr. Bennet stood in conversation, the bitter hostility that had marked their earlier exchange giving way to a shared concern for Elizabeth's health. An uneasy silence fell until Mr. Jones finished his examination, and Sally, the maid, opened the door and asked them to enter the room. The two men returned to Elizabeth's side, witnessing the apothecary instructing the distraught young lady. The apothecary spoke with a measured tone.

"Miss Bennet, you will need rest and care. Your face and throat will need weeks to heal, as will the injury to your head. Try not to speak. All the injuries are serious, but you should recover with time. The abrasions on your hands must be cleaned and wrapped for at least two days. You have a severe concussion; however, the laceration is not deep, but it could become infected. Under my direction, Sally has shaved a portion of your hair away from it to keep it clean. I am leaving a salve to promote healing. The bandages on your head must be changed thrice daily for the next week. I insist you stay in this room, staying in bed until I deem you well enough to leave it. You may experience mild to extreme dizziness for months. Consider yourself lucky to be alive."

Elizabeth nodded, wincing when the movement sent a sharp pain throughout her head, her gaze again finding Darcy's.

"Mr. Darcy, thank you," Elizabeth whispered.

Darcy offered a small, genuine smile. "Consider it a debt repaid for the joy your company brings. Sleep well, Miss Elizabeth." He bowed and left the room, leaving the Bennets alone with the apothecary and the maid.

As the door closed, Mr. Jones turned to Mr. Bennet. "Sir, your daughter must stay here while she recovers. Her concussion is severe, and the laceration on the back of her head will need particular care. It would be best if someone remained with her through the night to ensure her comfort and health. Do you wish to notify your family of Miss Elizabeth's condition? I can take a message to Longbourn since it is on my way to Meryton."

Mr. Bennet, his concern etched on his face, spoke slowly. "I will stay here with Lizzy tonight, and since Mr. Darcy assigned Sally to meet her needs, there is no need to bring anyone here from Longbourn until tomorrow. You need not take a message. I will send a note to my wife explaining my absence. As always, you have my gratitude, Mr. Jones."

With a final nod, Mr. Jones gathered his medical supplies and headed to the study, where he examined and treated Mr. Darcy's injuries before returning to his home in Meryton.

As Mr. Bennet settled into the chair beside Elizabeth's bed, she tried to adjust to a more comfortable position, pointing a wagging finger at her father; she rasped, "Papa, I may be injured, but I'm not dead. You must include me in conversations about my health."

Mr. Bennet sighed, looking guilty. "Forgive me, Lizzy. It's just... seeing you like this, it shakes a father."

"Papa," she began, her voice a stern whisper, "I appreciate your concern. But I need to know what happened. How did Mr. Darcy come to my rescue? What happened after Mr. Wickham dropped me? Why are we at Netherfield?"

Mr. Bennet sighed deeply, his gaze fixed on the floor. "Mr. Darcy heard your screams; stopped that scoundrel, Wickham, from doing any more harm to you. Colonel Fitzwilliam intercepted Wickham as he fled the scene and took the scoundrel to Meryton; the blackguard is sitting in a cell facing the consequences of his actions."

Elizabeth winced at the mention of Wickham, thankful for Darcy's intervention. "Papa, what of Mr. Darcy? Why did he come back to Netherfield? Who is Colonel Fitzwilliam? Are the Bingleys here?"

Her father hesitated, his fingers absentmindedly tapping on the chair's armrest. "I do not know why he came back to Netherfield. He saved you, and we owe him a debt of gratitude. Colonel Fitzwilliam is Mr. Darcy's cousin. The Bingleys are not here."

Elizabeth studied her father's face, searching his eyes to discover if he was being truthful. "Papa, I always thought Mr. Darcy was proud and disdainful, but in that moment, he risked himself for me. He must have a good heart."

Mr. Bennet somberly nodded. "I owe him an apology; my attitude upon first seeing him was poor. We will talk about what happened later. My priority is your recovery, Lizzy."

Elizabeth reached for her father's hand, offering a weak smile. "Yes, Papa. I am grateful to be alive."

Mr. Bennet's gaze softened as he gently held Elizabeth's bandaged hand. "Lizzy, try to rest. You are safe here. Mr. Jones said you need time to heal your throat. Please, stop talking and close your eyes," he whispered gently.

Elizabeth managed a weak smile, her gratitude evident in her tired eyes. She mouthed the words, "Thank you, Papa."

Eventually, Elizabeth restlessly slumbered, and her father reflected on his many deficiencies. He was completely ashamed of himself for failing to send a footman to escort Elizabeth and her sisters whenever they went out walking, for ignoring an urgent message from a neighbor, and for sitting by the fire reading while Elizabeth was lying unconscious at Netherfield. As the night progressed, the coals in the fireplace continued to cast a warm glow in the room, providing warmth but no comfort.

While Elizabeth spoke with her father, Darcy sat alone in his study, the door wide open. Lost in thought, his eyes fixed on a glass lamp that protected one large candle's steady flame from the puffs of air circulating the room; he sat there waiting because Richard sent a note from Meryton that gave an approximate time of arrival for himself and the militia commander, Colonel Forster.

There was a loud knocking on the front door at the expected time. For the first time that day, the butler could escort guests to the study and introduce them. Richard entered first, his countenance strained. Colonel Forster followed closely behind, his expression grim.

"Darcy," Richard greeted, nodding at his cousin as he entered the room. "I trust you are holding up well after these sad events."

Darcy rose from his chair, acknowledging Richard with a nod. "Cousin," he replied, his tone heavy with fatigue. "Thank you for your help. It would have been far worse without your assistance."

Richard waved off the gratitude. "No need for thanks, Darcy. We are family, and family watches out for each other. Now, tell us the full account of what happened."

Richard's jaw tightened with each detail as Darcy recounted the events leading to Elizabeth's rescue. Colonel Forster listened intently, his features reflecting his outrage.

"And Wickham ran straight into the arms of Colonel Fitzwilliam?" Colonel Forster inquired, breaking the momentary silence that followed Darcy's narrative.

Darcy's eyes hardened. "Yes, Richard detained him and took him to you in Meryton. I hope Wickham is now under lock and key either in the local jail or the brig. I have made it clear that I expect justice to be served."

Colonel Forster nodded approvingly. "He is in the brig guarded by two dependable men. That miscreant has caused enough trouble in Meryton. He will face harsh consequences for his actions."

"Thank you both for your support," Darcy said, looking at his cousin and Colonel Forster. "We must ensure Miss Elizabeth's safety and see this matter through. I am grateful to have you by my side in this endeavor. Her father is with her now, but I doubt he will be helpful since he rarely concerns himself with his daughters' lives."

Richard clapped Darcy on the shoulder. "You are not alone in this, Darcy. We will see it through together."

Mr. Bennet, having overheard the last part of the conversation as he entered the room, stepped forward, his expression worried. "Darcy, I may have been remiss in my duties as a father, but I am willing to do whatever it takes to ensure my daughter's health."

Darcy acknowledged Mr. Bennet's words with a stiff nod, appreciating the change in tone. Richard clapped Darcy on the shoulder once again. "Everything will be fine, Darcy. Miss Elizabeth will recover."

Having nothing further to say, Colonel Forster wished no part in a conversation that included the indolent Mr. Bennet.

"Gentlemen, I trust you have matters well in hand. Darcy, should you need assistance from me or the militia, do not hesitate to send word. Lieutenant Wickham will receive the punishment he deserves. However, I must see Miss Elizabeth to verify her injuries."

After a brief argument with Mr. Bennet, Colonel Forster was escorted to the guest chamber and allowed to view the slumbering lady. A glance at the bruised, bandaged woman was enough to determine that the lady was grievously injured. Colonel Forster retreated from the doorway, gave Mr. Bennet a final bow, and swiftly left the house.

Mr. Bennet, though late to the discussion, was resolved to play a more active role in his daughter's life. He returned to the study to speak with Darcy and Colonel Fitzwilliam.

"Mr. Darcy," Mr. Bennet began, "I must express my gratitude for your intervention. It seems my failings as a father have been laid bare, and I must rectify the errors of the past for the sake of Elizabeth's health."

Darcy acknowledged Mr. Bennet's words with a brisk nod. "Mr. Bennet, our priority now is to ensure Elizabeth's safety and help her recover. The past can be addressed another time."

As they spoke, a silent understanding passed between the men, a shared commitment to the well-being of Elizabeth Bennet.

Chapter 3

On Christmas Day, snow cascaded from the sky, covering Hertfordshire. The fields and towns wore a glistening white blanket of the powdery substance. However, the atmosphere within the estate's walls was far from festive. Elizabeth had developed a high fever during the night, leaving her restless and sweaty. The maid attending to her had sent word to Mr. Bennet requesting aid.

Mr. Bennet knew that Elizabeth's condition required more than his own limited knowledge, and so, with a heavy heart, he sent for the rest of his family and Mr. Jones.

Soon, the quiet entry hall of Netherfield was filled with the commotion of the Bennet family's arrival. Mrs. Bennet, flustered and concerned, hurriedly led Jane, Mary, Kitty, and Lydia into the house. The two youngest girls chattered nervously, aware they had abandoned Lizzy to run into Meryton the previous afternoon instead of gathering greenery for decorations.

As the Bennet women entered, the contrast between the joyful anticipation of Christmas at Longbourn and the somber reality within Netherfield was stark. There were no festive candles, no yule log burning, no smell of baking pies, nothing but an overwhelming dreariness.

Darcy and Richard, unprepared for the sudden invasion, exchanged uneasy glances. When the matriarch greeted them loudly, Darcy introduced his cousin to the Bennet women and turned to guide them to the parlor.

"Darcy, Colonel Fitzwilliam, this is an unexpected pleasure," Mrs. Bennet loudly exclaimed, "But where is Mr. Bingley? Where is Lizzy?"

Darcy cleared his throat, realizing he needed to address Bingley's whereabouts because Mr. Bennet had failed to do so.

"Mrs. Bennet, there has been a misunderstanding. Mr. Bingley returned to London after the ball last month for personal and business reasons and has decided to terminate his lease. The Netherfield Park lease is now in my name. He will not be returning."

Mrs. Bennet's eyes widened with shock, and her hands fluttered nervously. "Lease in your name? But what about his marked attention to Jane? Why would Mr. Bingley leave so abruptly?"

Darcy hesitated, then continued, "Mrs. Bennet, Mr. Bingley's circumstances have changed, and he found it necessary to stay in London. I did not press him with questions."

The news hit Mrs. Bennet like a blow; her distress was unmistakable. The younger Bennet sisters exchanged curious glances while Jane visibly paled, all her hopes of Bingley's return dashed to smithereens. Jane's face, once filled with hope, now wore an expression of disappointment, and the younger Bennet sisters exchanged worried glances.

Colonel Fitzwilliam interjected, attempting to steer the conversation away from the awkward topic. "Mrs. Bennet, our primary concern is Miss Elizabeth's health. She has developed a high fever, and we are awaiting Mr. Jones's arrival for an updated assessment."

Mrs. Bennet's attention shifted to her ailing daughter, and her anxiety deepened, as did the histrionics.

"Oh, Lizzy! My poor, dear Lizzy! So vexing! Always getting into a scrape! She has no consideration for my poor nerves! But we must do everything we can to nurse her back to health. Mr. Darcy, Colonel Fitzwilliam, you must help us! Jane, I need my salts! I feel palpitations in my chest!" These proclamations were accompanied by a waving handkerchief and swaying.

Jane and Mary jumped into action, taking the matron's arms to steady her and leading her to a chair before Jane produced a vial and held it under Mrs. Bennet's nose. Kitty and Lydia giggled at their mother's antics, knowing the woman must always claim center stage.

Darcy, realizing the situation was degrading into a farce, wanting to stop Mrs. Bennet's comments and save the two older ladies further embarrassment, nodded solemnly. "Mrs. Bennet, we will do everything in our power to assist Miss Elizabeth and provide the support your family needs during this challenging time."

Just as he finished speaking, the doorknocker sounded. The butler opened the front door and ushered in Mr. Jones. Mrs. Bennet jumped up and hurried toward him, her eyes wide with concern.

"Mr. Jones, how is my Lizzy? Please tell me she will be well again!" Mrs. Bennet implored.

The apothecary, shedding his outerwear, was taken aback by this unexpected greeting and looked grave as he responded, "Mrs. Bennet, Miss Elizabeth is indeed unwell. The fever has taken hold, and she requires immediate attention. I will do my best to alleviate her suffering, but she needs constant care. Perhaps one or two of your daughters can nurse her?"

Mrs. Bennet clutched at her chest, her eyes welling with tears. "Oh, my poor Lizzy! This is too much to bear!"

Darcy stepped forward, placing a reassuring hand on Mrs. Bennet's arm. "Mr. Jones, spare no expense on procuring whatever medicines and resources are needed. We are committed to Miss Elizabeth's recovery. We are willing to host Miss Bennet, Miss Mary, and Mr. Bennet until Miss Elizabeth fully recovers. You specified last night that she must avoid loud voices and noise."

The apothecary nodded in acknowledgment, and glancing at Mrs. Bennet, he cautioned, "Miss Elizabeth must not be upset during her recovery if she survives this fever. Anyone who cannot remain silent in her presence will be evicted from the room. Am I clear?"

Mrs. Bennet responded, "Perfectly clear, Mr. Jones. I believe that Jane, Mary, and I will accompany you." Her determined stare at Mary indicated that her middle daughter must follow her up the stairs to see Lizzy.

The atmosphere in Elizabeth's room was tense. Elizabeth lay in bed, her face flushed with fever and beads of sweat glistening on her forehead. Mr. Jones, a thin man with a stern expression, immediately checked her pulse and asked the maid about the progression of Elizabeth's symptoms.

Mrs. Bennet, her nerves frayed, paced anxiously by the bedside, occasionally casting worried glances at her daughter. Her worry was indicated by the wild fluttering of a handkerchief through the air and muttered barely audible words. "So typical... traipsing through the woods... staying out in bad weather... so inconsiderate of my nerves... battered and bruised...my nerves, my nerves."

Mr. Bennet, though typically reserved, couldn't hide the concern etched on his face. He approached Mr. Jones, inquiring about Elizabeth's condition, ignoring his wife and her nerves.

"Mr. Bennet," said the apothecary with a furrowed brow, "Miss Elizabeth is suffering from a high fever. We must try to bring it down, but I cannot guarantee the outcome."

A heavy silence settled in the room as the gravity of the situation sank in. When Mrs. Bennet understood the severity of the situation, she shrieked, "Noooooooooooooooo! Make my child well!"

Mr. Jones faced her husband and commanded, "Get your wife out of here now. I will not have her disturbing Miss Elizabeth with this incessant caterwauling."

Jane and Mary helped their stunned father remove the matron from the room, leading her downstairs to the parlor where the others anxiously awaited Mr. Jones's return. Mr. Bennet returned to Elizabeth's room after determining that his daughters could handle their mother without his help.

As Mrs. Bennet and her daughters entered the parlor, Darcy attempted to leave the room but was detained when Mrs. Bennet loudly proclaimed, "Mr. Darcy, Colonel Fitzwilliam, I cannot bear the thought of losing a daughter; you must help her!" she pleaded, her theatrics momentarily subsiding into genuine concern.

Darcy nodded solemnly, saying, "Rest assured, Mrs. Bennet, we will spare no effort in assisting Miss Elizabeth's recovery. You and your younger daughters are welcome to visit Netherfield daily; however, we are understaffed. We can only provide a room for your husband and a shared room for Miss Bennet and Miss Mary. Please let us know if there is anything specific we can do to assist you and your family during this challenging time."

Mrs. Bennet, still clutching her handkerchief, nodded appreciatively, her eyes filled with gratitude. "Oh, Mr. Darcy, you are too kind. To think that we must endure such trials on Christmas Day! But, you know, my nerves must bear it."

On the other side of the room, the younger Bennet sisters, Kitty and Lydia, continued to exchange loud whispers and nervous giggles. Colonel Fitzwilliam stepped forward with a gentle smile, observing the two young ladies' unconcerned demeanor and wanting a private conversation with Darcy.

"Mrs. Bennet, your youngest daughters need you. They seem overcome by distress." The colonel guided the matron to her daughters, bowed, and returned to Darcy.

The cousins made a hasty retreat to the privacy of the study, where Colonel Fitzwilliam closed and locked the door. He moved to the window, perused the falling snow, and faced Darcy. "This situation has become more complicated than we anticipated. Bingley's sudden departure, Miss Elizabeth's condition, and now half the Bennet family residing at Netherfield... where will it end?"

Darcy sighed, his brow furrowed with concern. "Indeed, Richard. I had not foreseen these challenges when I came here to court Elizabeth. With Bingley gone and Elizabeth gravely ill, we must tread carefully. We must not allow Mrs. Bennet to reside here with the two youngest daughters. Those three are never calm or quiet. They would hamper Elizabeth's recovery."

Colonel Fitzwilliam nodded in agreement. "We must be cautious in handling Mrs. Bennet's inquiries about Bingley. And we must ensure that your Elizabeth's recovery takes precedence over all else."

Darcy ran a hand through his hair, his usual composure strained. "I am committed to Elizabeth's well-being but fear the complications may grow. We must proceed with care and address each challenge as it arises. We must speak with Mr. Bennet about managing his wife and youngest girls."

Colonel Fitzwilliam concurred, "Agreed, Darcy. Her well-being must be our top priority, which may mean delicately addressing the situation with Mrs. Bennet and the younger sisters."

Darcy replied, "I briefly spoke about the lack of prepared rooms and staff with Mrs. Bennet, but imagine she disregarded my meaning. Let's find Mr. Bennet."

As the two gentlemen left the study to find Mr. Bennet, they encountered Jane and Mary in the hallway. The two sisters looked worried but tried to maintain a semblance of composure. Their visit to Elizabeth's room left them frightened by her appearance. Both were determined to stay at Netherfield to nurse Lizzy.

"Mr. Darcy, Colonel Fitzwilliam," Jane greeted them, her voice filled with concern. "How did this happen to Lizzy? Our mother must not see her again. The house will be filled with hysterical screams during each visit."

Darcy offered a reassuring smile. "Miss Bennet, Mr. Jones is attending to her, and we hope for the best. Your presence and support are appreciated. We will discuss your concerns with your father and keep you informed."

Mary, who had quietly listened, added, "We are willing to assist in any way we can. Jane and I can help administer medicine, change bandages, or do anything required. She is our beloved sister."

"Thank you, ladies," Colonel Fitzwilliam reiterated, acknowledging their concern. "We will be addressing the situation, and your cooperation is vital during this challenging time."

Darcy and Colonel Fitzwilliam continued searching for Mr. Bennet while Jane and Mary returned to Elizabeth.

The cousins found Mr. Bennet in the library looking out a window, perhaps contemplating the dire events that had befallen his favorite daughter or simply counting the falling snowflakes.

"Mr. Bennet," Darcy began, "we appreciate your understanding and cooperation during this difficult time. However, we must discuss the arrangements for Mrs. Bennet and the two youngest Miss Bennets. Their exuberance may hinder Miss Elizabeth's recovery. Plus, as mentioned earlier, we are understaffed. Yesterday, we came on horseback. My London household was given time off for the holiday. My carriage, luggage, and valet will not arrive for three more days. Mrs. Nichols, the housekeeper here at Netherfield, is trying to recruit staff, but the Bingleys left a poor impression with the servants."

Mr. Bennet sighed, knowing the truth in Darcy's words. "You speak sense, Mr. Darcy. My wife and the younger girls can be... lively. I shall talk to them and arrange for them to come here for short visits once Lizzy is healthy enough to endure the noise."

"Thank you, Mr. Bennet. We want to ensure the best conditions for Miss Elizabeth's recovery," Colonel Fitzwilliam added.

When a random thought slid to the forefront of his mind, Mr. Bennet shifted his stance and looked intently at Darcy before demanding, "What did the Bingleys do to the staff?"

Darcy hesitated for a moment, choosing his words carefully. "Charles and I left for London the day after the ball. He had pressing business matters; thus, my visit ended. The Bingley sisters followed him to town two days later with their entire entourage. They did not leave on the best terms with the permanent staff. Both sides were displeased because packing an entire household is difficult even when proper notice is given. Miss Bingley sacked the temporary staff without wages or references, claiming they were incompetent and derelict in performing their duties. Mrs. Nichols is doing her best to rectify the situation and recruit temporary help, but it will take some time to convince people that I will not mistreat staff."

Mr. Bennet nodded thoughtfully. "I see. Well, we must manage with what you have. I will speak to Mrs. Bennet and the younger girls about visiting hours and minimal noise in the sick room. As Mr. Jones instructed, anyone being loud will be removed."

Colonel Fitzwilliam added, "We appreciate your cooperation, Mr. Bennet. Miss Elizabeth's recovery is our priority, and a quiet and peaceful environment will be crucial for her healing."

A concerned Mrs. Bennet, having overheard part of the conversation as she approached the library, entered the room and loudly cried, "What are you all discussing? How is Lizzy? I must see her at once!"

Darcy stepped forward, trying to calm Mrs. Bennet's anxiety. "Mrs. Bennet, Miss Elizabeth is in good hands. Mr. Jones, Miss Bennet, and Miss Mary are attending to her, and we are making arrangements to ensure her recovery is as comfortable as possible."

Mrs. Bennet's eyes widened with worry. "Arrangements? What arrangements? And where are we to stay? I demand answers!"

Mr. Bennet stepped in, gently guiding his wife to a nearby chair. "My dear, we must consider what is best for Lizzy. Mr. Darcy and Colonel Fitzwilliam are taking steps to ensure a conducive environment for her recovery. You and our two youngest daughters will stay at Longbourn. We cannot leave our staff without a mistress."

Darcy added, "We have discussed the need for a quiet atmosphere, and Mr. Bennet has agreed to arrange visiting hours for you and the younger Miss Bennets once Miss Elizabeth is well enough. As for accommodations, we will arrange for Mr. Bennet, Miss Bennet, and Miss Mary to stay here."

Mrs. Bennet, although still worried about her daughter, seemed somewhat appeased by the assurances. "Well, I suppose that will have to do. But I must see Lizzy again. Take me to her at once!"

Darcy nodded, realizing that Mrs. Bennet's insistence was fueled by genuine concern. "Of course, Mrs. Bennet. We will escort you to Miss Elizabeth's room. Please do not cry out loudly when you see her."

As they made their way to Elizabeth's room, Darcy, Colonel Fitzwilliam, and Mr. Bennet attempted to prepare Mrs. Bennet to see her ailing daughter, cautioning her to whisper.

"Mrs. Bennet," Darcy began gently, "Miss Elizabeth has endured a great deal. She is resting now, and the environment must remain calm and quiet for her recovery. Please refrain from any loud exclamations or expressions of distress that might agitate her. Try to keep your voice very low."

Mrs. Bennet nodded solemnly. "I understand, Mr. Darcy. But you must assure me that Lizzy will recover. Those bruises may mar her forever. Oh, my poor nerves, how is this to be suffered?"

Darcy responded, "We are doing everything possible to ensure Miss Elizabeth's recovery. Mr. Jones is a skilled apothecary, and with the care and attention she is receiving, we hope for the best outcome."

As they reached the door to Elizabeth's room, Mr. Bennet opened it, revealing the quiet chamber where Elizabeth lay flanked by her two sensible sisters. The flickering light of a bedside lamp cast a gentle glow over her face, showing signs of her struggle with Wickham. The bandages on her head and hands were shocking proof of the dire state of Elizabeth's health. Mrs. Bennet gasped softly but managed to stifle any loud outbursts when she saw the purple bruises around her daughter's throat.

"Lizzy, my dearest Lizzy," she whispered, her voice heavy with worry. This time, the sight of her injured daughter, helpless and feverish, a stark contrast to the vivacious Lizzy she knew, did not result in a call for her salts.

Mr. Jones, who was adjusting bandages and checking Elizabeth's temperature, acknowledged their presence with a nod. "Mrs. Bennet, your daughter is resting. Please keep the noise to a minimum and limit your visit to a few minutes."

Despite her shock, Mrs. Bennet sank onto the chair beside the bed with relief that her daughter was alive. The matron reached out to touch a finger to Elizabeth's forehead, discovering the heat of the fever that gripped her daughter.

Mrs. Bennet murmured, "Lizzy, my dear, Mama is here. You must get well soon. We cannot have a sickly daughter on Christmas!"

Everyone stood back, allowing Mrs. Bennet a moment alone with her daughter. They observed the poignant scene as Mrs. Bennet clasped Elizabeth's bandaged hand, her eyes brimming with tears.

After a few moments, Mrs. Bennet turned toward the gentlemen, her voice shaky. "She looks so frail. What happened, Mr. Darcy? Tell me everything."

Darcy took a measured breath. "Mrs. Bennet, your daughter encountered George Wickham in the woods. He attacked her, and she fought him; Elizabeth sustained injuries. I came upon the scene and intervened. She is now under Mr. Jones's care, and we hope for her swift recovery."

Mrs. Bennet's eyes flashed with a mix of shock and anger. "Lieutenant Wickham? How could he? And where is he now?"

Colonel Fitzwilliam said, "Wickham is in custody, awaiting justice for his actions. He will face the consequences for what he has done."

Mrs. Bennet, though distressed, seemed satisfied with the news of Wickham's capture. "Good riddance! That man deceived us with his tales of woe. What fools he must have thought us!"

Mr. Bennet stepped forward, placing a comforting hand on his wife's shoulder. "Let us trust Mr. Jones and our daughters to care for Lizzy. She needs our support and a calm environment for her recovery."

Colonel Fitzwilliam reiterated, "Mrs. Bennet, we have arranged for Mr. Bennet, Miss Bennet, and Miss Mary to stay at Netherfield. We believe this will ensure a suitable environment for Miss Elizabeth's recovery."

Mrs. Bennet nodded, her focus returning to her daughter. A horrified shudder shook her body when she realized her daughter was ruined. The scoundrel's failure to complete his goal meant nothing. The whole family would be disgraced unless a suitable husband could be found.

"Yes, yes, anything for Lizzy. I will go home to Longbourn, but you must inform me about her condition. And I will visit daily."

Darcy assured her, "You will be kept informed, Mrs. Bennet. We all want what is best for Miss Elizabeth. Now, let us allow her to rest."

As everyone except Jane and a day maid left Elizabeth's room, Mrs. Bennet cast a lingering, worried glance at her daughter as the door closed softly. She clutched her husband's sleeve, pulled him aside, and stepped close.

"Husband, she is ruined. We'll be ostracized. Our daughters will never find husbands. What will happen to them?" whispered a distraught Mrs. Bennet.

Mr. Bennet looked at his distressed wife, his usually indifferent countenance now reflecting concern. He touched her shoulder gently and spoke softly, "My dear, our first priority is Elizabeth's recovery. We cannot allow ourselves to be consumed by worry over societal opinions. We must focus on supporting Lizzy and ensuring her well-being."

Mrs. Bennet, however, continued to fret, her mind racing with the potential consequences. "But the scandal, Mr. Bennet! What will become of our other daughters? How will we secure advantageous matches for them? Our family will be ruined!"

Mr. Bennet sighed, realizing the weight of the situation, and astounded his wife saw the potential harm to the family's reputation. "Yes, Fanny, this is undoubtedly a difficult circumstance. We must carefully consider our actions and find a way to manage the consequences. Do not mention anything about these events to anyone. Impress your daughters with the need for secrecy. But, for now, let us concentrate on Elizabeth's recovery. Once she is well, we can plan accordingly."

With a determined look, Mr. Bennet continued, "Darcy and Colonel Fitzwilliam have offered their assistance, and we will navigate through this together. Our daughters' futures are not entirely lost; we will find solutions. We must stay composed and handle this situation carefully."

Mrs. Bennet, though still anxious, nodded reluctantly, realizing the wisdom in her husband's words. "You are right, Mr. Bennet. Lizzy's health comes first. We must trust that, with time, we will find a way to manage the aftermath of this unfortunate incident."

The guestroom at Netherfield became a sanctuary where Elizabeth Bennet, weakened and frail, fought against the grip of the fever that had taken hold of her. Day turned into night as Mr. Jones and her sensible sisters, Jane and Mary, attended to her with unwavering dedication.

As the battle for her life continued, the news of Elizabeth's illness and the circumstances surrounding it remained carefully guarded. Mrs. Bennet and her youngest daughters continued their daily routines at Longbourn, maintaining an outward semblance of normalcy. Mrs. Bennet, true to her determination for prudence, refrained from revealing the details of Elizabeth's condition to her other daughters.

Meanwhile, Darcy and Colonel Fitzwilliam took it upon themselves to manage the delicate situation. They coordinated with Mr. Bennet daily, ensuring that the necessary arrangements were made for Elizabeth's care and the comfort of her family. The challenges extended beyond the physical realm; the potential impact on the family's reputation was imminently concerning.

In the quiet moments between consultations with Mr. Jones and the discussions with the Bennet family, Darcy reflected on the unforeseen turn of events. His initial desire to pursue Elizabeth had led to unexpected trials, testing the limits of his resolve. Darcy's focus shifted from courtship to a lifelong commitment to Elizabeth. He prayed that the second Bennet daughter would recover soon.

New Year's Day approached, but there was little festive spirit within the walls of Netherfield. The solemnity of Elizabeth's sickroom contrasted sharply with the holiday cheer that usually accompanied the season. The house remained undecorated, the flickering candlelight a muted reminder of the joy that eluded the estate's occupants.

Jane and Mary continued caring for Elizabeth, taking shifts to ensure their sister was never alone. Darcy would visit and read from a volume of Shakespeare's sonnets, knowing Lizzy would enjoy listening to them while Richard conversed with Jane or Mary about the war with France.

As the days passed, a tentative stability settled over Netherfield. Elizabeth's fever showed signs of relenting, and Mr. Jones cautiously expressed optimism about her recovery. However, the shadows under Lizzy's eyes were a silent testament to her inability to enjoy a restful sleep.

Mr. Jones continued daily visits, monitoring Elizabeth's progress and adjusting her treatment accordingly. The departure of her fever on December 28th marked a significant milestone, and the sight of Elizabeth awake and partaking in a simple meal brought a sense of relief to her family.

Meanwhile, Darcy and Colonel Fitzwilliam, in collaboration with Mr. Bennet, navigated the aftermath of Wickham's crimes. Wickham's disgraceful actions left a trail of financial and social chaos, with unpaid merchants and families with ruined daughters seeking restitution. Colonel Forster found himself inundated with unpaid bills, promissory notes, and demands for satisfaction. A search of Wickham's quarters revealed stolen items from fellow officers, compounding the charges against him.

The court-martial proceeded swiftly with so many charges filed against him that it was unnecessary to mention Elizabeth Bennet. On December 29th, George Wickham faced the consequences of his actions. The sentence was passed and carried out three hours later: death by firing squad. The disgraced officer departed the realm of the living, bringing closure to the Bennets and the Darcys.

New Year's Eve arrived, marked not by celebrations but by the silent acknowledgment of the passage of time. In the quiet moments before the clock struck midnight, the occupants of Netherfield clung to the belief that with the turn of the year, Elizabeth's condition would continue to improve, dispelling the shadows that had settled over their lives.

Chapter 4

The first light of New Year's Day bathed Netherfield in a soft glow, symbolizing the beginning of a new chapter. Within the walls of the estate, cautious optimism prevailed. Elizabeth's resilience and strength during the first week of her recovery hinted at the possibility of a brighter future.

The quiet corridors, which had witnessed the trials of the past week, now echoed with a tentative sense of hope. Elizabeth's ongoing recovery became a focal point, a testament to her determination and the support of those around her. Her hands and head were no longer bandaged, and a lighter shade and some yellow replaced the deep purple of the bruises.

Family members took turns sitting by Elizabeth's bedside, offering encouragement and support. The house, once silent, began to stir with the subtle sounds of everyday life resuming as the household staff was hired. Colonel Fitzwilliam and Darcy slowly rectified the harm done to the estate during Bingley's tenure.

Darcy spent hours reading to Elizabeth and her attending sister. In contrast, Mr. Bennet spent his days at Longbourn, only returning to spend the night at Netherfield, thus proving to Darcy that the patriarch was incapable of changing his indolent ways.

"Lizzy, how are you this morning? Is there less pain when you move your head?" Jane's furrowed brow belied her pleasant tone when talking to her sister.

An exasperated sigh later, Lizzy replied," I feel better daily. I can move my head slowly without a single twinge. I wish to get up. I want to walk. There's nothing wrong with my legs."

Jane pointed at the prone figure on the bed, waggled her forefinger from side to side, and replied with a teasing smile.

"No, Lizzy. You cannot go for a walk. Darcy's family physician is coming tomorrow. Maybe you can convince him to let you out of this room since Mr. Jones will not."

"But it's the first day of 1812! I want to greet the year standing up! This is unfair."

Jane laughed, a sweet tinkling sound that filled the room with merriment. Molly, the nurse who replaced the maid during the day, chuckled. Finally, Lizzy, eyes dancing with delight, raised both eyebrows, gave Jane a piercing look, and said, "Fine. You must carry me on your back if I cannot walk!"

"Oh, Lizzy. You are too big for that. You're not two years old anymore. You always wanted a piggyback ride, even when you were six!"

At the outraged expression on Elizabeth's face, Jane flung herself into a nearby armchair, covered her face, and burst into unrestrained laughter.

Quietly reading by the window, Darcy couldn't help but join in the laughter that filled the room. The carefree exchange between the sisters provided a welcomed respite from the recent somber atmosphere.

As the laughter subsided, Elizabeth turned her attention to Darcy, her eyes sparkling with mischief. "Mr. Darcy, you see the injustice I endure at my sister's hands. Surely, a walk on the first day of the new year is not too much to ask."

With a playful glint, Darcy replied, "Miss Elizabeth, I am afraid I must side with your sister on this matter. Dr. Witherspoon will be here tomorrow, and we must follow his advice. We wouldn't want to jeopardize your recovery."

Elizabeth feigned a dramatic sigh. "Very well, Mr. Darcy. But mark my words when Dr. Witherspoon gives permission, I shall take the longest and most delightful stroll through Netherfield Park."

Still recovering from her laughter, Jane said, "And I will be right there with you, Lizzy, to ensure you don't attempt any stunts that might impede your healing."

Their banter continued, creating an atmosphere of camaraderie and lightness. Darcy found himself enjoying these moments, realizing that laughter and shared humor were powerful healers in their own right.

As the clock ticked away the hours until tea, Darcy, Jane, and Elizabeth found solace in each other's company. Arriving just as the tea was placed on the table, Richard and Mary joined them. Afterward, the group took turns reading poetry until Elizabeth fell asleep. The promise of a new year began to take root, bringing the hope of brighter days ahead.

Mr. Bennet returned from Longbourn in the evening to find everyone gathered for a simple yet heartfelt New Year's celebration in Elizabeth's room. With a modest meal and a shared sense of gratitude, they welcomed 1812 with a newfound appreciation for the bonds that held them together. The shadows of the past days began to fade, making way for the dawn of a year that promised healing, growth, and the strength to face whatever challenges lay ahead.

The New Year's celebration in Elizabeth's room marked a turning point for the occupants of Netherfield. The shadows of recent challenges began to recede, replaced by a shared determination to embrace the possibilities that 1812 held.

Dr. Witherspoon, the Darcy family physician, arrived and confirmed her progress. He prescribed a gradual increase in activity, allowing short walks within the confines of the room. Elizabeth eagerly embraced these small freedoms, relishing the opportunity to move beyond the confines of her sickbed. In the days that followed, Elizabeth's recovery continued steadily.

The atmosphere at Netherfield lightened further as the three sisters spent more time together with Darcy and Richard. Reading sessions, quiet conversations, and shared laughter became a daily occurrence. Even Mr. Bennet, typically inclined toward solitude, was drawn into their circle. He found staying at Netherfield was more intellectually stimulating than reading alone in his Longbourn bookroom.

As Twelfth Night approached, Darcy became increasingly captivated by Elizabeth's resilience and spirit. Undiminished by recent events, her wit and humor became a source of constant delight. Their interactions evolved into a dance of shared glances, exchanged smiles, and a growing understanding that exceeded mere companionship.

One morning, Elizabeth, supported by Darcy, took her first tentative steps beyond the confines of her room. The corridors of Netherfield became a symbol of her journey from weakness to recovery. Observing her progress, Darcy marveled at her strength.

"Miss Elizabeth, get a firm grip on my arm. We'll be going to the end of this hallway today unless you wish to stop sooner," murmured Darcy.

Elizabeth wanted to walk but knew her body was unwilling to cooperate with her mind. She closed her eyes to force the wave of dizziness away. This weakness would be conquered. The hall came into focus when she opened her eyes.

"Don't worry, Mr. Darcy. I have no plans to swoon today." Elizabeth's playful tone belied the weak state of her body. She looked up and discovered his eyes darkening with concern.

He replied, "Do not worry about swooning. I'm quite good at catching you when you stumble."

"Yes, you've proven yourself adept at saving me. I've been wondering why you came back to Netherfield. Will you share your reason with me?" Elizabeth looked up at him, one eyebrow raised.

Darcy shrugged, a tint of red rising above his cravat. Maybe it was time to share his hope that she would become his wife. Perhaps she was more amenable to the possibility of a shared future. He squared his shoulders and patted the hand resting on his arm.

"Miss Elizabeth, I returned for several reasons. I needed to correct the poor impression I made upon entering the neighborhood. The thought of allowing the good citizens of Meryton to be fleeced or abused by Wickham ate at my conscience. Colonel Fitzwilliam accompanied me to speak with Colonel Forster about the rake's proclivities. And..."

A feminine gasp interrupted his words. He looked down and saw Elizabeth's fearful expression. The mention of Wickham still caused her to quake with dread. He patted her hand and whispered, "Elizabeth, you are safe. Wickham is gone forever. I will not allow anyone to harm you again. You are safe."

Stammering, Elizabeth responded, "Please...this is ridiculous...I know he is dead... I..." unable to continue, she hung her head and gripped his arm tighter. Her indomitable spirit rose, and she raised her head. "I refuse to live in fear. I will conquer this. Please, what other reason did you have for returning to Netherfield?"

Darcy, recognizing the vulnerability in Elizabeth's eyes, softened his gaze. "Miss Elizabeth, you have my word that Wickham's actions will fade from your mind. However, if you allow me to do so, I promise to protect you from similar men. As for the other reason, it is more personal. I missed your company and could not dismiss my desire to be near you, hear you speak, see your lips smile in delight, watch you blush when complimented, and engage with you in a lively debate."

Elizabeth's eyes widened at his admission, and she couldn't help but be moved by the sincerity in his words. "Mr. Darcy, your candor surprises me. You truly came back for me?"

Darcy took a moment before responding, "In the time we've spent together, I've come to value your intelligence, wit, inner strength, and honesty. I find myself drawn to you, Miss Elizabeth, in ways I hadn't anticipated. Since your arrival here, those feelings have grown into a deeper sentiment that I cannot ignore."

He paused, searching her eyes for a sign of her thoughts. "I returned to Netherfield hoping that you might be open to a more permanent connection between us once I'd proven myself worthy of your regard. I wanted to call on you, court you, and marry you."

Shocked by his confession, Elizabeth let the words hang in the air momentarily. She pondered the sincerity in his eyes and the kindness he had shown her during her recovery. A faint smile played on her lips as she said, "Mr. Darcy, your honesty is refreshing. I appreciate your regard; your company has brought comfort during these trying times. My opinion of you has greatly improved. I enjoy your company, intelligence, honesty, and steadfast support. The thought of a shared future is appealing."

The air between them seemed to shift as they walked down the corridor. There was a shared understanding that the journey they had embarked upon was one filled with possibilities. The halls of Netherfield, once a symbol of recovery for Elizabeth, now held the promise of a new chapter in her life—one intertwined with the enigmatic Mr. Darcy.

Chapter 5

Mrs. Bennet descended upon Netherfield with the two youngest daughters dressed in their finest apparel to celebrate Twelfth Night at Netherfield with the rest of her family. She greeted Darcy and Richard loudly.

"La, there you are! Two fine gentlemen willing to hold a celebration just for us! Where is my Jane? Oh! There she is by the refreshments. We can't stay long. Sir Lucas hosts the whole neighborhood tonight, and we must go there or be considered rude!" The matron moved away on her last pronouncement, hardly giving the men a chance to bow or speak.

Richard burst into a loud guffaw as the woman sought Jane, rushing past Mary, Elizabeth, and Mr. Bennet, who sat together near the fireplace on a comfortable damask sofa. Kitty and Lydia gave hurried curtsies and scampered after their mother, having learned the cousins were immune to their coquetry.

In a low voice, Richard confided, "There go three of the silliest women in England. Thank heaven we won't need to entertain them for long."

Darcy shrugged, smiled at the sentiment, and responded, "Yes, it seems the three eldest daughters received their father's intelligence while the two youngest did not garner an ounce of it."

Richard chuckled at Darcy's dry humor. "Indeed, Darcy, it is a wonder how the same parents can produce such different offspring. Mr. Bennet's wit skipped the younger ones. It seems Mrs. Bennet's nerves and fancies have taken root in Lydia. The contrast between Jane and Elizabeth and their younger sisters is stark."

Darcy nodded in agreement. "It's a curious thing, indeed. Nature has its way of distributing qualities among siblings. They are quite a handful, but we should be thankful for small mercies. At least, Mrs. Bennet's visit will be brief, and we can resume some semblance of normalcy afterward."

As Mrs. Bennet continued to bustle around, exclaiming over the decorations and the refreshments, Mr. Bennet joined Darcy and Richard with a sardonic grin. "Gentlemen, I hope you appreciate my sacrifice by allowing my wife and the younger girls to grace you with their presence. A visit from Mrs. Bennet is always a test of one's patience."

Richard chuckled, "Your forbearance is commendable, Mr. Bennet. We are grateful for your family's company on this Twelfth Night. As you know, Elizabeth wished to celebrate the evening with all of you."

Meanwhile, Mrs. Bennet approached Jane, who was quietly observing the lively gathering.

"Jane, my dear, stand up straight and smile. You must make an impression. There are two eligible gentlemen here. You cannot afford to be overlooked!" Mrs. Bennet whispered in a tone that was far from discreet.

Jane, ever composed, offered a serene smile. "Mother, we are here to care for Lizzy, not to secure husbands. Tonight, we enjoy the festivities."

Mrs. Bennet huffed. "Well, it wouldn't hurt to keep an eye out, would it? Now, let me see you sparkle!"

Elizabeth and Mr. Bennet shared a knowing look as they observed the spectacle. Still recovering but eager to participate, Elizabeth told her father, "It seems Mama is determined to showcase Jane tonight."

Mr. Bennet raised an eyebrow. "Yes, it appears so. Let her have her fun. Twelfth Night is meant for merriment, after all."

Darcy and Richard found themselves caught up in the lively atmosphere, observing the varying degrees of enthusiasm displayed by the Bennet sisters. Amid the celebration, Elizabeth exchanged amused glances with Darcy, silently acknowledging the absurdity and charm of the Bennet family dynamics.

When the clock struck eight, Mrs. Bennet declared that she and her youngest daughters must depart promptly to attend the gathering at Sir Lucas's residence.

Darcy and Colonel Fitzwilliam bid farewell to the Bennet matriarch and her youngest daughters. A sense of calm settled over Netherfield as the door closed behind them.

Mr. Bennet, looking more amused than ever, remarked, "Well, that was an adventure. I hope you gentlemen survived with your sanity intact."

Darcy chuckled, "Barely, Mr. Bennet. Your youngest daughters are quite spirited."

Mr. Bennet's eyes twinkled. "Yes, they are. Now, let us enjoy the remainder of the evening without the theatrics of my dear wife and the younger Bennets."

As the lively Twelfth Night celebration continued, Darcy conversed with Elizabeth. Her recovery was progressing well, and she radiated a vitality that contrasted with the subdued atmosphere of the past twelve days. Her bruises had faded but were still discernable under the cleverly applied makeup.

"Miss Elizabeth," Darcy began, "how are you finding the festivities? Is the merriment to your liking?"

Elizabeth smiled. "It is delightful, Mr. Darcy. I had almost forgotten what it felt like to be surrounded by such cheer. My recovery is slow, but tonight is a welcome reprieve. Thank you for carrying me down the stairs."

Darcy nodded, his gaze lingering on her. "I am pleased to see you in good spirits. Twelfth Night is a time for joy and celebration. I hope the coming days bring more reasons for happiness."

Colonel Fitzwilliam joined them as they conversed, adding his observations about the evening. The camaraderie between the three of them created a warm and congenial atmosphere. They engaged Mary and Jane in the conversation, leaving Mr. Bennet, seated nearby, to observe the scene with a satisfied smile. The burdens of the recent events seemed to lift, if only for a moment, as laughter and light-hearted banter filled the room.

As the clock struck midnight, signaling the end of the festive gathering, Darcy rose and extended a hand to Elizabeth. "Miss Elizabeth, may I have the honor of escorting you back to your room?"

She accepted with a gracious smile, and together, they made their way through the quiet halls of Netherfield until they reached the grand staircase. Without hesitation, Darcy scooped Elizabeth into his arms and carried her up the stairs before depositing her slight form on the landing, ensuring her feet were steady.

Chapter 6

As the days passed, the halls of Netherfield echoed with the sounds of Elizabeth's footsteps, a testament to her improving health. Darcy often accompanied her on these walks, providing a steadying presence as she regained her strength. The quiet conversations during these strolls allowed them to share their thoughts and dreams.

One sunny afternoon in late January, as they wandered through the halls, Darcy spoke earnestly, "Miss Elizabeth, these past weeks have been a journey for my soul. I hope for a future where moments of joy and tranquility are always present. I would be honored if you would consider sharing that future with me as my wife."

Elizabeth's heart skipped a beat, and a warmth spread through her. She met Darcy's gaze, finding sincerity in his eyes. "Mr. Darcy," she replied softly, "I, too, have contemplated the future. Your presence has been a source of strength and comfort. I believe that, together, we can face whatever challenges come our way."

"I cannot bear the thought of you leaving me, Elizabeth. The hours I spend writing business letters and overseeing this estate are torture. The separation is bearable only because I know Jane and Mary are with you, making you smile, helping you exercise, and reading to you. When the doctor deems it safe for you to travel, we will broach this subject again. For now, let us enjoy each moment we spend together."

In the evenings, Darcy continued to read amusing novels to Elizabeth, whose vision still blurred at times, their companionship fostering a connection greater than friendship. At the same time, Mr. Bennet sat nearby in a favorite armchair, listening to the story and drinking brandy. The library at Netherfield became a sanctuary where words and emotions intertwined, creating a space for understanding and intimacy.

One evening, Darcy closed the book they had been reading with a snap; he looked at Elizabeth with a sincerity that reflected the depth of his feelings and leaned closer. He whispered, "Miss Elizabeth, I love you most ardently. I wish to be your husband, your protector, your children's father, the knight who always rescues you from harm. I cannot wait for the doctor's prognosis any longer. Will you marry me?"

Elizabeth, moved by his words, nodded. "Mr. Darcy, your presence has brought light to my darkest hours. I have fallen in love with you and welcome the prospect of a shared future. Yes, I will marry you!"

A joyous smile spread across Darcy's face as Elizabeth's words sank in. He held her hand gently, savoring the moment. "Elizabeth, you have made me the happiest man alive. I promise to be the husband you deserve, to cherish and protect you for all our days." He brought her hand to his lips and placed a kiss upon it.

Mr. Bennet cleared his throat, eyes dancing with glee, and said, "So, you've finally come to the point. I thought you'd never get around to declaring yourself."

Mr. Bennent rose from his chair and approached the couple, kissing his daughter's cheek and shaking Darcy's hand. Afterward, he went to the door and firmly closed it. When he turned, all vestiges of humor were gone; his expression was grim.

"Darcy, now that you will become my son, you will tell me why Mr. Bingley abandoned my Jane."

Elizabeth interjected, "Papa, that hardly matters. You can't force Mr. Darcy to tell us such a personal thing."

"Elizabeth Rose Bennet, you may hold sway over your concerns but not mine. The abandonment of Bingley haunts my eldest daughter. Miss Bingley's lies in her letter to Jane wounded my dear girl. I want answers, and I want them now. Do not pretend your indifference to the knowledge." Mr. Bennet's flinty gaze rested on Darcy.

Darcy took a deep breath before responding. "Sir, I assure you that my friend Bingley's actions were unplanned. Miss Bingley and her sister orchestrated a scheme to separate him from Jane. They sought to undermine his affection for her, painting an unfavorable picture of your daughter's feelings, labeling her a heartless fortune hunter. The shrews tried to enlist my aid in the scheme, but I declined. If we are to discuss this matter, it would be best if Jane and Mary join us."

Mr. Bennet's face darkened as he absorbed the revelation. Elizabeth's eyes widened in shock, and she glanced at her father. The sisters were summoned to join the discussion. Colonel Fitzwilliam saw the ladies heading toward the library and followed them.

The colonel entered the room on the heels of the ladies, pausing briefly in the doorway to catch Darcy's eye. "Well, this is a fine collection of Bennets to behold. Is a lowly colonel welcome to join the party?"

A chorus of greetings indicated he could join them. At Darcy's slight nod, Richard entered the library and locked the door, saying, "A meeting like this demands privacy. Shall we all move closer to the far fireplace? I haven't learned to fully trust servants as the ones in my father's house stand outside doors attempting to hear our conversations."

After everyone settled comfortably at the room's far end, Mr. Bennet explained why the ladies were summoned to attend the meeting without mentioning the engagement. Jane looked down at her hands to hide her displeasure. In her mind, there was no excuse for Mr. Bingley's permanent departure from the neighborhood in such an uncivil manner, and she no longer wished for his return. Seeing how Mr. Darcy and Colonel Fitzwilliam behaved opened her eyes to the many improprieties in the Bingleys' behavior toward everyone.

Darcy continued, "Mr. Bingley was deceived into believing that Jane did not return his affections. The Bingley siblings took advantage of his trusting nature. He was devastated when he discovered the manipulation that had occurred, but it was too late. One of Miss Bingley's wealthy friends, Miss Constance Barrow, compromised him at a ball a week after he went to London, convinced by Caroline Bingley that Charles secretly admired her. Bingley deeply regrets the pain he unwittingly caused Jane, but he was forced to marry Miss Barrow three weeks later."

Mr. Bennet, though visibly angered by this betrayal, managed to maintain composure. "So, it was a vile plot against my daughter's happiness and their brother's future by the Bingley sisters. They thought themselves clever. What actions have you taken, Mr. Darcy, to set this right?"

Darcy replied, "There is nothing I can do to help my friend. I told Mr. Bingley all I knew about his sisters' schemes, and he severed all ties with them. Miss Bingley's scheming has not gone unnoticed by society, and it has caused her a considerable loss of standing. Mr. Bingley is now determined to nurture his slight regard for his bride and win his wife's favor. Otherwise, his future life will be miserable. He is too ashamed to write to you, Mr. Bennet. He gave up the lease because he couldn't bear to return here with his wife. He felt it would hurt Miss Bennet."

"I do not wish to correspond with the weak-willed ninny. My Jane has escaped joining herself to a man controlled by the whims of his sisters." The stern proclamation issued by Mr. Bennet surprised everyone.

Jane reached into her pocket and produced a worn letter, which Miss Bingley wrote two days after the Netherfield Ball. She handed the missive to Darcy. "I believe you need to see this. Miss Bingley mentions your sister is expected to marry Mr. Bingley with your approval and a forthcoming engagement to herself." Jane folded her hands in her lap and waited as the people surrounding her burst into speech.

Darcy's eyes widened as he read Miss Bingley's letter aloud. The revelation that she intended to manipulate Georgiana into an engagement with Mr. Bingley, with the expectation of Darcy's approval, left him both angered and appalled. The room erupted into a chorus of exclamations as the gravity of Miss Bingley's schemes became evident.

Elizabeth's eyes flashed with a mixture of concern and indignation. She exclaimed, "It is as I said, Jane. The woman was not your friend. She told you lies."

Mr. Bennet's face darkened with anger. "The audacity of that woman! To think she could meddle in the affairs of so many people in such a manner is beyond belief."

Mary, usually reserved, spoke with a stern tone. "Such deceit and manipulation are grievous offenses. I trust that justice will be served in this matter."

Colonel Fitzwilliam reflected on the letter. His voice boomed with rage. "This letter is beyond reprehensible, Darcy. Miss Bingley's actions are a threat to your family. To use your sister's future happiness as a pawn in her schemes to capture you is unconscionable. Bad enough, she used her to break Miss Bennet's heart. To imply your happiness at such an engagement... is unbelievable! This perfidy must be addressed decisively."

Darcy, his jaw set in determination, folded the letter and looked at Jane. "I am grateful to you for bringing this to my attention. Miss Bingley's schemes will not go unpunished. My fifteen-year-old sister has been at Pemberley since last October with her companion. There was never any possibility of a match with Charles Bingley. I will take additional steps to ensure my sister's safety, and my staff will be instructed to bar the Bingleys and Hurst families from my homes. I must distance myself from them and hold Miss Bingley accountable for her words and actions. However, Mr. Bennet has some happy news to share with you."

Caught off guard, Mr. Bennet glowered at his soon-to-be son-in-law. "Yes, indeed. Excellent news. Elizabeth has agreed to marry Mr. Darcy."

Everyone rushed to congratulate and well-wish the happy couple. Miss Bingley's deceit was temporarily forgotten. After celebratory drinks were shared and the ladies began discussing wedding plans, the men escaped to the study, where a resolute Darcy started writing letters to keep his sister safe from the machinations of a social-climbing harpy.

In the following days, Darcy and Richard took action to ensure Georgiana's safety. Arrangements were made to restrict the access of the Bingleys and Hursts to Darcy's properties.

The Earl and Countess of Matlock took the story of Miss Bingley's treachery to the highest echelons of society. They ensured that the truth about Miss Bingley's nefarious plots reached every corner of the ton. The consequences were severe and immediate. Society firmly closed its doors to those who sought to manipulate and deceive.

Miss Bingley's standing crumbled as her deceit became common knowledge, resulting in her being ostracized from respectable social circles. The shame and scorn heaped upon her proved a formidable punishment, tarnishing her reputation irreparably. Caroline Bingley gave up her dreams of rising into the upper echelons of society. Instead, she traveled to New York City, where she planned to find and marry a man who was more appealing in looks and wealth than Fitzwilliam Darcy. Unfortunately, her reputation as a deceitful shrew followed her across the ocean. She learned frugality and lived a lonely yet comfortable life as a spinster in a small western town called Aberdeen.

Having severed all ties with his scheming sisters, Mr. Bingley and his wife, Constance, were left to build a life as a couple. Though disappointed in Bingley's initial lack of love, Constance affectionately showered Charles with attention. She saw the potential for a happy marriage with the young man and encouraged him to relocate to Scarborough, where his other relatives and factories were situated. Within a few months, Charles reconciled to the marriage and developed a fondness for his wife that eventually grew into love.

Mrs. Hurst shared her sister's fate. The Matlocks ensured society learned of her complicity in the harmful machinations against a country gentleman's daughter. Mr. Hurst, a gluttonous man with a resentful temper, shared the repercussions. The diminishing invitations and icy receptions the couple received left the Hursts scorned by polite society. After throwing Caroline out, Mr. Hurst packed up his household, sold the townhouse, and retreated with his wife to his father's estate, where he could shoot birds and hunt in peace. Mrs. Hurst, wishing to garner acceptance from her in-laws, learned to think before speaking, ignore her sister's letters, and cater to her husband and his parents.

Georgiana, who despised Miss Bingley, was distressed upon learning of the woman's manipulations. The young lady was learning that many people were not honest or kind. Darcy's letters reassured her of his unwavering support and protection, shared the news of his engagement, and promised to send Richard to fetch her to attend the wedding scheduled for Valentine's Day.

Chapter 7

The days leading up to the wedding were a flurry of activity. Netherfield bustled with excitement as preparations were made to celebrate the union of Mr. Darcy and Miss Elizabeth Bennet.

Mr. Jones was pleased with Elizabeth's health and cautioned the couple to avoid traveling in a carriage for more than four consecutive hours on adequately maintained roads. He warned, "If she experiences head pains or dizziness, no matter how slight, she must seek an inn and rest for at least a day." His demeanor stiffened as his piercing gaze caught Darcy's brief smile.

Herding Darcy away from Elizabeth, he soundly chastised the young man. "Mr. Darcy, when I say rest, I mean she must lie down and sleep. No physical activity of any kind. If she cannot sleep, read to her. Her head must be kept as still as possible. Do you understand my meaning, sir? Take a supply of the ingredients for willow bark tea and a jar of honey along. It will help relieve her pain."

A chastened Darcy sheepishly agreed with the apothecary before returning to Elizabeth.

After Mr. Jones left, Mr. Bennet appeared, signaling for the young man to follow him. Mr. Bennet led Darcy to the stables, navigating around the stalls to the tack room, where he indicated that Darcy should close the door.

Mr. Bennet wasted no time broaching a subject Darcy had fervently hoped the man would forget. Darcy leaned against the wooden wall of the enclosed space, lips pressed firmly together.

"Explain to me clearly and without prevarication why you took over the Netherfield lease. No more delays or excuses, son."

"I took the lease primarily because I wanted to court Elizabeth. Bingley came to my London house raging about his predicament, how he must marry some woman due to a compromise, expressing his dashed hopes of living in Hertfordshire and the cruelty of his sisters when they shut the house down and fired the servants without compensating them. He was looking at a substantial financial penalty for abandoning the lease. While I could not help him with the compromise, I was able to help him avoid the penalty by assuming the rest of the lease. However, I clarified that he must repay me for compensating the servants whom Miss Bingley cheated."

Darcy began to pace in the small space, running his fingers through his hair and blinking back the sudden moisture in his eyes. "I have been attracted to a few women in the past years, but never did I consider marriage to one of them. After my infamous behavior at the Meryton assembly, I began to watch Elizabeth whenever we attended the same function. I dreamt of her holding my child on the lawn at Pemberley each night. Sometimes, it was just one babe; other times, she was surrounded by several urchins, smiling and laughing, calling me to join them. How could I ignore my heart?"

Mr. Bennet stared at Darcy, incredulous. The younger man was everything good and kind. This man would care for his daughter and be there for the entire family in body and spirit. Darcy saw the older man's expression and coughed.

"I offered to purchase the lease because I had to return to Elizabeth. Plus, I needed to rectify the situation the servants were enduring after being callously dismissed without compensation. Bingley never gave their situation a thought. I stayed in London long enough to settle some business matters. I begged Colonel Fitzwilliam, who was on extended medical leave due to injuries sustained in battle, to help me with the mess awaiting me in Meryton. Have you any more urgent questions?" Darcy was tired of justifying his return to Mr. Bennet. It was distressing to remember the month he was in London, the loneliness and sense of dread. He fervently hoped Mr. Bennet would stop quizzing him on the subject.

Mr. Bennet shook his head, and the men silently returned to the house. Darcy immediately went to find Elizabeth while Mr. Bennet went to secure his favorite chair in the library. The sound of laughter filtered into the room as the Bennet ladies continued to decorate the house for the upcoming nuptials.

Netherfield was filled with joy and festivity on Friday, February 14, 1812. The drawing rooms of Netherfield were adorned with flowers, and the fragrance of fresh blooms from the Darcy hothouse in London wafted through the halls. Friends and family gathered, their faces lit with smiles and good wishes for the couple.

The ceremony occurred in the beautifully decorated front parlor, with Mr. Bennet proudly escorting his daughter down the aisle. A radiant Elizabeth exchanged vows with Darcy, their promises sealing a union forged through calamity and strengthened by love.

The gathered guests, including the Bennets, the Gardiners, the Philips, Colonel Fitzwilliam and his parents, and Georgiana Darcy, witnessed the union with heartfelt joy. After the ceremony, the newlyweds and their guests enjoyed a festive reception with music, dancing, and a sumptuous wedding feast.

As the festivities progressed, Darcy and Elizabeth shared their first dance as husband and wife. It was a waltz. The first notes of the melody reached their ears, and as they moved together, the room seemed to fade away, leaving only the two of them in a world of their own. The newlyweds found themselves swept away by the music.

Darcy held Elizabeth with a tenderness that spoke volumes. He looked into her eyes, his gaze reflecting the depth of his feelings. Remembrances of the challenges they had overcome, the shadows of the past, and the uncertainty of the future seemed to dissipate in that moment.

Each step they took was a testament to the resilience of their love, a love that had weathered storms and emerged victorious on the other side. Elizabeth felt a profound connection with Darcy, her heart beating harmoniously with the music.

Usually composed and reserved, Darcy allowed himself to be vulnerable in that dance. In the intimacy of the steps, he silently conveyed his gratitude for the light Elizabeth had brought into his life. The promise of a shared future echoed in every movement, a promise that went beyond the spoken vows they exchanged.

As the dance ended, Darcy held Elizabeth a moment longer as if savoring the culmination of their journey. In their quiet gaze, there was an unspoken acknowledgment of the deep love that had guided them from darkness to this moment of shared joy. With a final, lingering touch, they stepped back, the world rushing back around them. The room erupted in cheers and applause, but in the hearts of Mr. and Mrs. Darcy, a dance had just concluded that resonated with the echoes of their shared history and the promise of an enduring future together.

The following day, the couple set off for Pemberley, the grand estate that held the legacy of the Darcy family. While Pemberley represented their future, Netherfield remained an indelible part of their history. It had weathered the storm of adversity, standing strong against the darkness cast by the actions of malicious individuals. And it belonged to them.

Chapter 8

After Elizabeth agreed to marry him, Darcy bought Netherfield. It would be an excellent place for the Darcys to stay when visiting the Bennets. Plus, it would provide shelter for the Bennets if a disaster at Longbourn occurred. In the interim, Jane and Mary accepted an invitation to stay at Netherfield under the watchful eye of their father and a middle-aged female companion. The companion would instruct them in art, music, and the etiquette displayed in London drawing rooms. The ladies would be presented at court during the upcoming season, allowing them to attract men of worth, men who would love and cherish them.

As Mr. and Mrs. Darcy departed for Pemberley, Mr. Bennet watched their carriage leave. His emotions were a mix of pride, nostalgia, and a hint of melancholy. The responsibility of caring for Netherfield, in addition to Longbourn, rested squarely on his shoulders. As the carriage disappeared, he sighed, knowing his life would change significantly. He decided to transfer his collection of books to Netherfield's library, providing him a quiet haven for reading without disturbances caused by nerves.

Mrs. Bennet, though prone to dramatics, was surprisingly composed as the carriage disappeared from view. Elizabeth's marriage brought a sense of accomplishment. Yet, a flicker of concern crossed her face. The thought of her daughter's new life and the responsibilities Mr. Bennet now bore settled on her mind, and she couldn't help but worry about the future of her four unmarried daughters.

An hour later, Mr. Bennet watched another carriage, surrounded by guards, carry Colonel Fitzwilliam, his parents, and Georgiana Darcy to London, where they would stay for a month before taking Georgiana home to Pemberley. Mr. Bennet would miss those leaving but welcomed the chance to care for Netherfield with the Darcy steward's help. Before entering the house, he briefly wondered what the passengers would do in London. He pushed the thought aside; his immediate concern was gathering his wife and two youngest children together for the short trip to Longbourn.

Colonel Fitzwilliam's journey to London with his parents and Georgiana was bittersweet. As he glanced out of the window, he pondered the recent past. His protective instincts kicked in, particularly for Georgiana, and he couldn't shake the feeling of responsibility for her well-being. His parents' support was evident, yet he was Georgiana's legal co-guardian and responsible for her safety. Thoughts of Miss Bingley's malevolence lingered in the back of his mind.

The Earl and Countess of Matlock exchanged glances. While proud of their son's decisiveness and commitment to family, there was a shared concern for the challenges ahead. The social repercussions of Miss Bingley's deceit and the possible impact on Georgiana's reputation needed addressing. As the carriage rumbled on, they shared a silent determination to guide their family through the upcoming trials.

Looking out the window at the barren countryside, Georgiana reflected on her life. The prospect of attending a few events in London made her smile, but the shadow of Miss Bingley's schemes still haunted her thoughts. With a resolve unusual for the young lady, she promised herself that, come what may, she would face the challenges ahead with grace and resilience. As the carriage carried her away from Netherfield, she clutched a small heart-shaped pendant…a gift from her brother…as a source of comfort.

Two weeks after the wedding, Mr. Bennet informed his wife that the two youngest girls would return to the schoolroom. Mrs. Bloom, a highly recommended governess, would be arriving to teach them proper behavior and the skills that gentlewomen must possess. Mrs. Bennet's initial reaction was a mix of surprise, fury, and trepidation. Introducing such a figure into the household without her knowledge! How dare he? Her concerns about the potential sternness of the governess clashed with the hope for refinement she envisioned for her two youngest daughters.

Kitty and Lydia, unaware of the coming change, awoke to the sounds of their mother's exclamations. The news hit them like a sudden storm. Wide-eyed and curious, they exchanged uncertain glances. The prospect of structured lessons and the looming presence of a new authority figure sparked excitement and apprehension in their young minds.

When the governess entered Longbourn, a tall woman with stern features, Mrs. Bennet braced herself for the impact of this new presence. The atmosphere in the house seemed to shift as the governess took charge, setting expectations and routines. Mrs. Bennet, though initially hesitant, observed the woman's methods with a keen eye.

Kitty and Lydia, with their usual disregard for authority, tested the waters of this new arrangement. Their reactions ranged from attempts at charm to overt resistance. The governess, a seasoned figure accustomed to managing the education of brash young ladies, met their antics with a firm but fair hand. Mrs. Bennet, watching this dynamic, found herself admiring the woman and began to sit in on the lessons.

As Mrs. Bloom began to instill a sense of order and purpose in the following weeks, Mrs. Bennet observed a transformation in her younger daughters. The initial chaos gave way to a structured routine, and Kitty and Lydia's once unpredictable energy found a channel in their studies. While still prone to moments of fretful concern, Mrs. Bennet recognized the positive impact the governess had on her daughters and herself.

As Jane and Mary settled into their new rooms at Netherfield, the prospect of a companion to guide them in high society's arts and etiquette filled them with anticipation and curiosity.

For Jane, the arrival of a companion meant an opportunity to refine her social graces and artistic abilities in an establishment away from Longbourn. She envisioned herself learning the intricacies of polite conversation, mastering the art of the fan, and honing her skills in music. Jane asked her father to arrange a time for a servant to bring her harp to Netherfield. Jane's innate kindness and grace made her an ideal candidate for acceptance in London. She was excited by the thought of entering London society with newfound poise and hoping to attract a man of substance who would appreciate her gentle nature.

Mary saw the companion's arrival as a chance to broaden her intellectual horizons. She eagerly anticipated discussions on religion, literature, philosophy, and the arts. Mary hoped to make a meaningful impression at court through her knowledge and insightful conversations, seeking a match who shared her intellectual pursuits and appreciated her quiet depth.

Their father observed the proceedings with amusement and concern. While he appreciated the opportunity for his daughters to receive guidance and refinement, he worried about London's societal expectations and potential pitfalls. Nevertheless, Mr. Bennet acknowledged that Jane and Mary deserved every chance to find happiness in a world that placed great importance on appearances.

Mrs. Starch, the companion, arrived two days after Darcy and Elizabeth departed. Jane and Mary engaged in lessons that extended beyond the academic. They learned the intricacies of navigating the complex social landscape, the art of small talk, and the importance of making a favorable impression. Jane's warmth and Mary's intellectual prowess complemented each other, creating a harmonious atmosphere within the halls of Netherfield.

As the days turned into weeks, Jane and Mary, under the guidance of their companion, blossomed into refined young women capable of taking London by storm. The upcoming London season held the promise of new beginnings and the potential for love. Netherfield, once touched by illness and shadows, now echoed with the laughter and aspirations of Jane and Mary, a testament to the enduring spirit of those who forged a path leading to newfound possibilities.

Chapter 9

December 1822 - Epilogue

Snowflakes danced in the wintry air, creating a serene tableau around Netherfield. The estate, once touched by shadows and uncertainty, now stood as a testament to enduring love and the resilience of the human spirit. Christmas at Netherfield had become a cherished tradition for the Darcy family. The practice began in 1812 and carried on for every following year.

As the three Darcy carriages approached the grand entrance, Elizabeth was engulfed by a cascade of memories. The contagious laughter of their children, the comforting warmth of shared moments, and the echoes of a life intricately intertwined. She found solace in the gentle pressure of Darcy's hand, a silent acknowledgment of the profound love that had weathered trials and triumphs.

"Here we are, Elizabeth, back at Netherfield for another Christmas. It feels like a lifetime since our first dance in the ballroom. You spent the dance chastising me about my lack of conversation." The slight upturn to Darcy's mouth and a teasing glint in his eyes softened the words.

Elizabeth turned to study the handsome man beside her, her heart warmed by the fondness in his eyes. After all these years, he still fixated on that dreaded ball. She thought it was time he released the haunting memories of that evening.

She offered him a tender smile and replied, "I think of our wedding waltz as the beginning of our ballroom dances. It was the most enchanting dance of my life at the time. We've shared many special dances, but that first one will forever be in my heart."

Darcy's smile deepened at her words. "You're right. Our wedding dance was magical. When we came to spend the Christmas season with your family in 1812, and you told me we would become parents, it was a dream come true." He drew her close, leaned down, and pressed a tender kiss to her lips, a silent celebration of the countless loving actions that had shaped their journey.

The halls of Netherfield were adorned with festive decorations, and their evergreen scent permeated the air. The family gathered in the grand drawing room, where a roaring fire cast a cozy glow. Mr. Bennet, now a jovial grandfather, sat in his favorite armchair, Bible in hand, surrounded by several grandchildren as he finished reading the story of the Nativity.

Mr. Bennet rose, his eyes lighting up as he shook Darcy's hand and embraced Elizabeth. "Ah, the Darcys have returned. Welcome back to Netherfield, my dears!"

Darcy smiled, "Thank you, Bennet. It's good to be with the family for the holidays."

A vibrant mix of personalities filled the room with exuberance. Four of the five Darcy children darted in, narrowly avoiding a collision with Mrs. Bennet in their rush to join their many cousins, barely managing a quick bow or curtsy before joining them. The eldest daughter, Anne, named in honor of Darcy's mother, was now seven. Mischievous twin boys, aged five, injected a whirlwind of energy into the household. At nine, the oldest son, Alexander George Darcy, was already eyeing a plate of strawberry tarts with a steady stare.

In the doorway, their nanny held the youngest child, a sleeping toddler of eighteen months, a precious daughter named Francine. Elizabeth gestured for the woman to take the child to the nursery. There would be plenty of time to let the little girl get reacquainted with her cousins in the next three weeks.

Anne squealed in delight, "Grandfather, look at the snow! Can we go sledding tomorrow if the snow is deep enough?"

Mr. Bennet patted the child's shoulder. "Of course, my dear. Netherfield's grounds are perfect for winter adventures."

In the corner, Jane and Mary, now married ladies with five children between them, conversed with Mrs. Starch, who had become a beloved fixture in the family, training the youngest girls when Mrs. Bloom departed Longbourn in 1814. She presided over the tea tray with a watchful eye, her features softened by her affection for the family she helped shape.

Jane was married to a successful London barrister and lived in town most of the year with her husband and three children. Mary married a physician whose London practice was flourishing. Their townhouse was not as large as Jane's home, but it was in the same neighborhood. Mary's two children, boys, were searching Netherfield for her husband in a game of hide-and-seek. Jane and Mary suspected both husbands were hiding in the billiard room where they could enjoy a brandy with the other men.

Near the tall windows, Lydia and Kitty stood talking about their plans to get together in the summer at Bath. They were constantly interrupted by three children who seemed to take turns pulling at their mama's hands, vying for attention while their husbands were across the room speaking with Mrs. Bennet. The two youngest Bennet daughters had married local men. Kitty had married John Lucas and lived with him at Lucas Lodge. Lydia had surprised everyone by falling madly in love with a solicitor whose practice was in Stevenage, a nearby town. Both women frequently visited Longbourn.

Sitting with his wife and three boys, Richard Fitzwilliam exchanged a knowing glance with Darcy, flicking his eyes to the other side of the room where his older brother, Sebastian Fitzwilliam, Viscount Sterling, conversed with his young wife. Darcy smiled broadly at the viscount, who proudly cradled his infant son in one arm while stroking the boy's cheek. Sebastian had been sent on a diplomatic mission to Italy in 1819, where he met and married a charming lady of noble birth. Now, at forty-two, the viscount had a wife and child.

Though aged, the Earl and Countess of Matlock beamed with pride as they observed their sons interact with the whole family. Sebastian had finally found happiness with a beautiful young woman, and Richard had astonished the family by securing the hand of Lady Emily Barclay, the Earl of Derby's only child. Richard's oldest son would eventually inherit his grandfather's title since it could be passed down through the female line. Richard lived with his thriving family on an estate named Mist Haven that he inherited from a maternal aunt, only twenty miles from Pemberley and forty miles from Matlock.

Richard stood to kiss Elizabeth's cheek and embraced Darcy in a brief hug. "Darcy, my favorite cousin, another Christmas at Netherfield. Who would have thought? Georgiana is upstairs resting while the new baby sleeps. I believe her husband is in the billiards room with Jane's husband. The men congregate there whenever they need to escape from playing games with the youngsters."

Darcy replied, "Indeed, Richard. It's become a tradition I wouldn't trade for anything. We've been talking about coming down earlier and staying longer to avoid the raging blizzards we've been getting at Pemberley during December and January."

The grand piano, a centerpiece in the room, resonated with music as Georgiana's daughter, Rose, played a festive tune. The older children gathered around the instrument, singing. Laughter and joy echoed through the room, filling Netherfield with the spirit of Christmas as the six-year-old girl entertained the gathering.

Tears of joy welled in Elizabeth's eyes as she surveyed the scene. One day, one of her boys would be the master of this house. She grabbed a tapered goblet and filled it with lemonade.

When the final notes of the music melted away, the grand room echoed with a resonant silence, a perfect prelude to the momentous words that followed. Elizabeth, her goblet raised high in a gesture of both celebration and reverence, proclaimed with a radiant smile, "A toast to Netherfield, where our love story began and continues to grow."

Swiftly, Darcy mirrored her gesture, lifting his glass and acknowledging her words. His deep voice resonated through the room as he declared, "To the family, love, and the enduring spirit of Netherfield." His eyes locked on Elizabeth's. In that gaze, a depth of emotion passed between them, a silent language shared by the couple. Darcy's eyes glowed with intense emotion, pride, and profound affection.

Elizabeth had chosen this moment, surrounded by the embrace of their extended family, to confirm a tender secret that bound them even closer. Only Darcy, attuned to the nuances of his wife's habits and choices, recognized the significance of her recent choice of beverage. She had been abstaining from wine, opting for lemonade. In this subtle toast, Elizabeth had communicated to him alone, amidst the familial revelry, that a new life had quickened, and a cherished addition to their growing family was on the horizon. Elizabeth's eyes sparkled with anticipation of a private celebration. Darcy's heart swelled with gratitude for the expanding tapestry of their love that Netherfield continued to witness.

Amidst the laughter, music, and camaraderie, the Darcy, Bennet, and Fitzwilliam families celebrated not just Christmas at Netherfield but a legacy of enduring love. The years had woven a rich tapestry of shared experiences, triumphs, and challenges, and Netherfield witnessed their journey. The scars of the past had become marks of resilience, and the love that illuminated the darkest corners continued to shine with the brightest light, a beacon of hope and happiness for future generations.

The End

Published Stories

- Born to serve
- Jane: A Born to Serve Bonus Chapter
- Dark Before Light
- Mistaken Heart, Revised
- The Right Choice
- Dancing & Pistols

Thank you!

Reviews help authors more than you might think.
If you enjoyed this story, please leave a positive review.

Don't miss out!

Visit the website below and you can sign up to receive emails whenever Linda Wagner publishes a new book. There's no charge and no obligation.

https://books2read.com/r/B-A-MHLOB-NGRND

BOOKS2READ

Connecting independent readers to independent writers.

Also by Linda Wagner

Dragons, Deceit, and Desire
Born to Serve

Standalone
Jane: A Born to Serve Bonus Chapter
Dark Before Light

About the Author

L. Wagner lives in Texas and is happily married to a wonderful man who indulges their cat with daily treats. She enjoys writing as a hobby and enjoys reading Pride and Prejudice variations, mysteries, paranormal fantasy, and science fiction.

A Pride and Prejudice fan since the 1960s, she finally decided to contribute a few stories to the JAFF community. Hopefully, the twists and turns of her imagination will interest you.

Milton Keynes UK
Ingram Content Group UK Ltd.
UKHW011256050724
445102UK00001B/37